IT'S ONLY THE END OF THE WORLD

For my son, the real Charlie Ray.
With grateful thanks to Eve, Samantha, Siobhan and Anne.

Kelpies is an imprint of Floris Books
First published in 2018 by Floris Books
© 2018 J.A. Henderson

J.A. Henderson has asserted his right under the
Copyright, Designs and Patent Act of 1988 to be
identified as the Author of this Work

The publisher acknowledges subsidy from
Creative Scotland towards the publication
of this volume

 Also available as an eBook

British Library CIP data available
ISBN 978-178250-517-4
Printed in Poland

IT'S ONLY THE END OF THE WORLD

J.A. HENDERSON

KELPIESEDGE

One Month Earlier

Gerry Ray's head shot up, penlight clenched between his teeth. One by one, the overhead lights were flickering to life.

"Someone's coming, Frankie!" he hissed. "I thought you were keeping a lookout!"

"My bad." A metallic voice crackled out of the computer speaker on a nearby desk. "Everyone makes mistakes, Gerry."

"Not a bloody Artificial Intelligence! You're supposed to be infallible."

"Well, that's nice of you to say, but I took myself offline while you corrupted Manticorps' databases. Y'know, in case you wiped me by mistake."

"I'm sorely tempted now. You said the place would be empty."

"It was when you broke in. Not my fault your sabotage is taking so long."

"What will I do?"

"You could always pretend to be the pizza delivery guy, but I'd suggest hiding."

Gerry crouched down in a corner, scrunched behind a chrome console, sweating face pressed against the cold metal.

A group of men and women in white coats made their way through the room, oblivious to his presence. The crowd were practically falling over each other to please a stout middle-aged woman marching in the centre. Small wonder. She was vice president of Manticorps and her foul temper was legendary.

"We've made another breakthrough in the Marginal Science Division, Mrs Magdalene," a tall man said excitedly. "What we've achieved is nothing short of extraordinary."

"That's vice president," the woman snapped. "And it better be or you'll regret dragging me out here at this time of night."

"We felt it best for you to witness the results in person." The lead scientist elbowed his companion out of the way. "Our new research is… eh… highly controversial. Not the kind of thing you can send an internal memo about."

"Make it quick then." Mrs Magdalene looked at her watch. "I've got tickets for *Wicked* and it starts in half an hour."

She pressed her pass key to the lock. The door slid open with a whoosh and the human convoy vanished into the corridor of Manticorps' Marginal Science Division.

Gerry Ray waited until they were well out of earshot. Then he scrambled to the nearest computer and began to type.

"Shouldn't you be escaping, Gerry?" Frankie asked. "This is no time to be posting your predicament on Facebook."

"As soon as the vice president of Manticorps and her research team reach their destination, they'll see we've ruined their precious research." Gerry finished with a flourish. "So I've overloaded the security systems in the east wing and shut the entire section down."

"You've done what?"

"It's fused the electronic doors." He grinned triumphantly. "They're trapped in their own labs."

"Then get out now," the voice said urgently. "I'll take it from here."

"They're not going anywhere." Gerry sprinted down the corridors and out of the building.

As he raced across the car park, there was a dull whump behind him. He skidded to a halt and turned.

A plume of smoke was billowing from the roof of the Marginal Science Division and he could hear muffled screaming from the flaming interior.

"Oh my God." Gerry Ray put a trembling hand to his mouth. "Frankie, what have you *done*?"

Part 1

The Shake-up

A lot of people try to shape the future.
Parents. Governments. Bankers.
The police. But it's the young ones
who live in it. And we will fight for it.

– Matt Wolf, *Teenage*

Charlie Ray huddled under the covers, listening to the stranger hiding in his cupboard.

He'd woken when he heard the window slowly slide up. The creak of a floorboard and the click of the cupboard door softly closing had convinced him he wasn't dreaming. Now a strange crunching noise emanated from inside.

He opened one eye and saw the digital clock read 3.00 a.m. Far too late for any of his friends to be playing a stupid prank. Anyway, he didn't have any friends.

Charlie lay perfectly still, pretending to be asleep, forcing his breathing to remain rhythmic. A month ago he would have pulled the pillow over his head and curled into a ball, hoping the intruder would leave him alone.

Not any more. These days, the only thing that scared Charlie was himself.

His mother was sleeping in the next room, but he had no intention of shouting for help. There was no way he was going to put her in any kind of danger. This was his problem and he would deal with it.

He remained motionless, calculating which object in his room would make the most useful weapon. There was a guitar on its stand by the window, a baseball bat leaning against the bookcase and a baseball Blu-Tacked to the second shelf. A heavy paperweight lay on his computer desk.

Charlie threw back the covers and rolled across the floor. He grabbed the bat and sprang to his feet, clutching it in both hands.

Pthhhhhp.

He blinked rapidly.

"You in there." He looked incredulously at the closed cupboard door. "Did you just…*fart*?"

"Couldn't help it," a muffled voice retorted. "I'm scrunched up like an accordion."

Charlie could see the key was still sticking out of the cupboard's lock, so he marched over and swiftly turned it. The handle rattled a few times then stopped.

"Uh oh."

"Yeah. You're trapped, whoever you are," Charlie announced. "Now I'm going to call the police."

"Good luck with that, buster," the voice scoffed. "Your phone is in here with me. I'm lookin at your photo gallery right now."

Charlie glanced at the desk. Sure enough, his phone was gone. "*Why?*"

"'Cause it's boring in the closet and I wanted to have some light entertainment while I ate my crisps. What's a prawn cocktail anyhow?" Charlie heard the sound of a packet being scrunched.

"I'm finished now," the voice continued. "So open this door or I'm gonna post that video you recorded of yourself singing along to Beyoncé in front of the mirror."

"Why are you doing this to me?" The boy's head was spinning. "Who *are* you?"

"Just let me out. I ain't gonna harm no one."

"I'm going to get my mum and she can call the police on *her* phone."

"You might find it a smidge difficult to rouse her," the voice said apologetically. "I was told to put a few sleeping pills in her hot chocolate so she wouldn't disturb us."

"You did *what*?" Charlie's jaw tightened. "Nobody messes with my mum. Not after all she's been through. Nobody!"

He unlocked the door and yanked it open, bat raised above his head.

A girl burst out of the darkness and crashed into him. Charlie landed on his back with a grunt, the intruder squarely on top.

"Surprise!" she giggled, then got quickly to her feet.

The boy stared in astonishment as she did an awkward little dance on the spot.

"Gotta go to the ladies' room," she gasped. "Had a whole bottle of Coke before I got here. 1.5-litre size."

"It's at the end of the landing." Charlie was too taken aback to say anything else.

"Back in two shakes." She hobbled out of the door. "Nice tartan PJs, by the way."

When she returned, Charlie had changed out of his pyjamas and was sitting cross-legged on the bed, tapping the baseball bat into his palm.

He studied the stranger carefully. She was a well-built girl with cold blue eyes and her round face was framed by a glossy shoulder-length bob. She wore a sparkly green top, short skirt and large black boots over crimson striped tights. He supposed she was quite pretty, in an odd sort of way, and looked about the same age as him.

"That's better." She grinned, revealing a huge gap between her front teeth. "I must have a bladder the size of a pea. Should have gone before I climbed up your drainpipe."

Her way of speaking was decidedly strange and reminded him of the old gangster movies his father, Gerry, used to watch. But he didn't like to think about his dad. Not if he could help it.

"Why were you in my cupboard?" he demanded.

"Nobody but you can know I'm here, see? I had to hide until I was sure your mom was out cold." The stranger shrugged. "'Sides, I thought it would be funny."

"Do I look like I'm laughing?"

"You sure don't seem the jolly type," the girl muttered. "I reckon your face would slide off if you tried to raise a smile."

"*Excuse* me?"

"The name's Daffodil McNugget." She held out her hand. When Charlie refused to shake it, she stuck a finger up his nose.

"Stop it!" He batted her away. "I want some answers or I *will* call the police."

"All right, grumpy." Daffodil backed off. "A voice in my head told me to how to find you, so I could pass on an important message. Happy now?"

"Well, that explains a lot." Charlie clutched the bat tighter. "Want me to whip you up a tinfoil hat?"

"Ooh. Is that what the in-crowd are wearin these days?" Daffodil glanced down at her clothes. "Only I reckon it might clash with my outfit."

"Oh, dear God."

"Relax, will you?" She rolled her eyes. "I'm only joshin."

"Stop 'joshin' and start explaining before I wallop you with this bat. Who the hell *are* you?"

"That's a real thorny subject. See, I don't actually *remember* who I am." Daffodil scratched her temple uncertainly. "In fact, I don't recall much at all."

"Is that why you made up such a daft name?"

"You're one smart cookie, Chaz!" She beamed. "Howd'ya figure it out?"

Charlie jerked his thumb at the bunch of yellow flowers his mum had plonked on the dresser to brighten the room. Next to it was an empty carton of Chicken McNuggets.

"Ah." Daffodil pulled a face. "That obvious, huh?" She shrugged. "Call me Mac if you like."

"There are several things I feel like calling you and 'Mac' is at the bottom of the list."

"All right grumpster." She looked at him quizzically. "Ain't you even a little curious about why I'm here?"

"I'd be a lot more curious if it wasn't the middle of the night." Charlie rubbed his eyes. Now that he could see the girl wasn't some robber, he was more annoyed than alarmed. "Right now, I'm leaning towards escorting you out the front door, using the toe of my boot. My neighbour has a four year old. Go hide in his wardrobe, if you're into that kind of thing."

"Wise guy, huh?" Daffodil adjusted her tights and smoothed down her skirt, while Charlie tried not to stare. "I already said I'm here 'cause I got a message for you."

"From an imaginary voice in your head."

"Nothing imaginary about it," she corrected. "He's called Frankie and he knows *everything*." Her voice lowered in admiration. "He told me what an accordion was and how to put pictures online. I should ask him about prawn cocktails next."

"The kid next door could tell you all that." Charlie pointed his bat at her. "Get out of my house. I won't warn you again."

"Whatever." Daffodil gave a disdainful sniff and turned to go. "But the message ain't from Frankie. It's from a guy called Gerry Ray."

Charlie was off the bed in an instant.

"Wait!" He grabbed her arm. "*What* did you say?"

"The message is from a guy called Gerry Ray," she repeated. "Hey. You both got the same last name! Is he some kinda relative?"

"Gerry Ray is my father." Charlie steered Daffodil to his computer chair and sat her down. When he let go, his hands were shaking. "And I haven't seen him since he walked out on us."

"I don't recall my own mom or pop," Daffodil said sadly. "So I've been makin up stories in my head about them. There's not a lot to do in a closet." She gave a heartfelt sigh. "I don't even know if they're alive or—"

"My dad up and left last month," Charlie interrupted. "Cleared out our bank accounts. Didn't say goodbye or even leave a note."

"Oh, I *do* apologise. I don't know what day of the week it is and had to make up a name for myself a minute ago. What am *I* complaining about?"

"Just give me the message." The boy held out his hand.

"Whatever you say. But I need a computer."

"Eh?" He pointed. "There's one next to your elbow."

"Oh, that's what the weird-lookin box is." Daffodil rested her hand on top of the PC and its screen lit up. "I'm still gettin used to new stuff."

"You didn't even switch it on." Charlie stared at her. "How is that possible?"

"Ain't got a clue. Didn't even know what a cell phone was till Frankie told me. He's the only way I find out anythin." She scratched her head. "Had to do a runner from the cab that brought me here 'cause I didn't know I was supposed to pay."

But Charlie wasn't listening. A familiar face had appeared on the monitor.

Gerry Ray was sitting attentively, hands clasped on his lap, as if he had been waiting there for some time. He looked nervous and exhausted. His normally neat hair was dyed platinum and he had a bushy moustache to match. His usual shirt and tie had been replaced by jeans and a yellow T-shirt, and he wore a bandana round his neck.

"Dad!" Charlie gasped. "It's really you! Where have you been?"

"I've got so much to say, my boy." The man smiled wanly. "And so little time to say it. But let's start with how much I love you."

"You got a funny way of showing it," Charlie shot back. "Mum's been in bits since you left. Me too, for that matter."

"I had no choice, son. I'm in hiding. It's the reason for this disguise."

"That's a disguise?" Daffodil sniffed. "I thought a seagull crashed into his face."

"Hiding from what?" Charlie pushed the girl away. "Unpaid parking tickets? You lived in a semi and still collected CDs." He glanced at the room next to his. "I should wake Mum."

"No!" His father held up a hand. "I have a story to tell you, but I need to make it quick. Frankie is jamming this signal, but every second I talk increases the chances the people bugging your house will grow suspicious."

"The house is bugged?" Charlie couldn't hide his disbelief. "That's crazy—"

"Son." Gerry Ray cut him short. "Please listen. All our lives depend on it."

That shut the boy up.

"A while ago, I stole something extremely valuable from some very nasty people and they'll do anything to get it back. That's why I had to go on the run."

"So return it," Charlie snapped. "I've been worried sick about you."

"I would if I could, but it's not an option. However, if they knew I'd been in touch, or even cared what happened to you and Mum, they'd take you hostage to flush me out of hiding." Gerry looked mortified. "I had to make it seem like I'd completely abandoned my family, for your own safety." His voice lowered. "Please. Let me tell you what happened. No interruptions until I'm finished."

"All right." Charlie gave a surly nod. "But this better be good."

"In our younger days, your mum and I were formidable computer hackers." Gerry tapped a finger to his nose. "Corporate raiders they called us, 'cause we used to break into big conglomerates and expose their dirty secrets anonymously to the press."

"Pull the other one, Dad. Do I look that naive?"

"Sure you want him to answer?" Daffodil asked innocently.

"Oh, we were the best. Until we had you, that is. Then we gave it all up, so our son could have a normal life. It's why we never said anything about our past." Gerry gave a pained smile. "But I suppose old habits die hard. A couple of months ago, I got a mysterious email about a defence company called Manticorps, especially one particular department: the Marginal Science Division. It seems their scientists had developed some kind of artificial intelligence they nicknamed 'Frankie'. Now they were using him to invent sinister new ways of waging war."

"Frankie?" Charlie looked at Daffodil in alarm. "He's a bad guy?"

"I didn't know that," the girl whispered. "He's got a nice voice."

"Frankie is short for Frankenstein. Some bright spark at Manticorps had a pretty warped sense of humour." They could see from Gerry's grim expression that he didn't appreciate the joke.

"Frankie had invented all sorts of terrible stuff for them. A drug called the Atlas Serum, which made soldiers stronger, more aggressive and resistant to injury or illness. Microchips implanted in their flesh, so Frankie could be downloaded onto them and communicate directly with troop leaders. Exoskeletons that turned men into walking tanks. New biological weapons to wipe out enemy forces." Gerry threw up his hands in disgust. "I had to do something about it. Your mum didn't like the idea, but I talked her into letting me investigate."

"Mum *knew* what you were up to?" The boy grasped the edge of his desk.

Your mother is a lot tougher than she looks.

"So what happened?" Despite himself, Charlie was fascinated by this new side to his father.

"I hacked Frankie, of course. Found out Manticorps had programmed him to do whatever they ordered. So I rejigged him to obey me instead." Gerry fiddled awkwardly with the bandana round his neck. "Then I had to get him out of the Marginal Science Division before Manticorps realised what I'd done and reset him."

"I don't understand." Charlie frowned. "If this AI is so dangerous, why didn't you just shut it down entirely?"

"His intelligence might be artificial, but it's real," Gerry scolded. "As far as I was concerned, Frankie was alive and I couldn't simply kill him." He stroked his moustache nervously. "Frankie shut down the building's security systems and let me in. I smuggled him out in one of their own military chips, then went back and wiped every piece of Manticorps research from their databases, including the cloud." He ran a hand down his face.

"While I was doing that, the entire research team turned up to show the vice president of Manticorps their latest development. I had to override the security systems and lock them in their labs, so I could escape." Gerry's lip trembled. "Only Frankie short-circuited the building and set it on fire. The scientists I trapped died of smoke inhalation." A tear slid down his cheek. "I didn't know he'd do something so extreme. I swear."

"So you destroyed your family and set free a monster just to relive your glory days? Is that what you're telling me?"

There was a crunching sound. Charlie was gripping the desk so tightly the front had fractured. Jagged splinters protruded from his bleeding fingers but the boy didn't seem to notice.

"That's solid wood." Daffodil's eyes widened. "How'd'ya manage to break it?"

"Frankie isn't free," Gerry went on obliviously. "While he was still under my control, I programmed him to never take another life or do anything to cause harm to a sentient being." He gave an exhausted sigh. "But the damage was done. Manticorps know only a handful of people on earth are capable of hacking Frankie, and I'm one of them. With their scientists dead and their research gone, they need the chip containing him so they can start again – and they'll stop at nothing to retrieve it."

"So where are you and Frankie now? And how come he's able to talk with Daffodil?"

"Daffodil?" Gerry looked surprised. "Is that what she's calling herself?"

"Feel free to enlighten me 'bout my real name," the girl grunted. "I seem to have forgotten it."

"Daffodil will do for now." Gerry rapped on the screen. "Kid? Lift up your hair and show Charlie your neck."

"What? That is beyond creepy."

"Please."

The girl reluctantly bowed her head. There was a small bulge at the base of her skull.

"See that little lump?" Gerry said. "It's the chip containing Frankie."

"Hey, buddy!" Daffodil sat up again. "I ain't at *all* comfortable with this. Who gave you the right?" Her icy eyes narrowed. "Is *that* why I don't remember nothin about my past? 'Cause the first thing I recall is standin in some room, dressed like a traffic light, with Frankie givin me directions to this place and a message for Chaz here. He promised to fill me in later, so I went along with it."

Charlie raised an eyebrow and she scratched her cheek awkwardly.

"Didn't realise he was a mass murderer at the time…"

"I can't give you the answers you want right now." Gerry looked abashed. "But I'll admit your memory has been messed up a bit."

"I'll mess with your face!" Daffodil raged. "What kind of monster are you, stickin something like that in my neck without askin first?"

"That is kinda crappy, Dad," Charlie agreed.

"You have to trust me, Daffodil," Gerry pleaded. "And you can do much more than communicate with Frankie. He can access any piece of technology for you. Security systems. Cash points. Databases. You have some incredible resources at your fingertips."

"OK. That does sound pretty cool," the girl admitted. "Even if I didn't understand a word you said."

"For a start, it meant you could give Charlie this message without it being intercepted," Gerry continued. "Manticorps' operatives will be watching the house, but hopefully, it will look like Charlie's finally found a girlfriend and she's sneaking in to visit him."

"Hey!" Charlie flushed. "What do you mean, *finally* found a girlfriend?"

"He means anyone who'd date you would have to be more desperate than a Mexican outlaw," Daffodil giggled. "You ain't exactly boyfriend material."

Charlie ignored her. "Why wait a month to contact me, Dad?"

"Frankie has been planning an alternative way to fight back against Manticorps' operatives. You know, now that he's not allowed to just kill them. We had to prepare a few things before we got you involved."

"Got *me* involved?" The boy gave a start. "I don't like the sound of that."

"Neither do I," Gerry said miserably. "But I'm no longer part of Frankie's scheme. If our family are ever to be together again, you're the one who'll have to destroy Manticorps." He looked pained. "It's a tall order, I admit. Those rogues have their own private army."

"Me?" Charlie goggled. "You do realise I'm only fourteen?"

"That's why Frankie and Daffodil are going to help."

"Great." The girl pouted. "Somethin else I wasn't consulted about."

"This is ridiculous!" Charlie stammered.

"Frankie says you have certain… abilities that will prove invaluable to him." Gerry clasped his hands together. "And his intelligence dwarfs ours. He doesn't make mistakes. Or… not often, anyway."

"I play the PS4 and watch Netflix, Dad." The boy folded his arms. "I always come fifth at sports. I'm not bloody Superman."

"I'll second that, Dumbledore," Daffodil added. "This kid ain't exactly the adventurous type."

"Dumbledore?" Charlie squinted at her. "You didn't know what a mobile was but you've seen the *Harry Potter* movies?"

"I've read the books, stupid. I'll explain later."

"My night is getting more and more surreal." Charlie turned back to the computer. "Are you sure about this, Dad?"

"Not at all. I wanted you kept out of the picture altogether, but Frankie insists you and… eh… Daffodil are the only people who can help him pull this off. How he intends to do it is a mystery to me, but apparently my interfering or giving you more information will disrupt whatever idea he's cooked up."

"What if that scheme involves me and Chaz getting killed, you hairy-nosed old goat?"

"Hey!" Charlie elbowed her in the ribs. "That's my father you're talking to."

"Look. I've used every safeguard I know to make Frankie incapable of harming anyone, and he's programmed to protect you both." Gerry still looked utterly wretched. "If you succeed in defeating Manticorps, I can come home. Frankie will show Daffodil how to remove his chip and we'll tell her who she is."

"Still don't see what's wrong with right now, bub."

"We have our reasons."

"And if your son fails?" The girl scowled. "'Cause it don't look like he can tie his shoelaces without a manual."

"Then we'll all be dead, so it won't matter." Gerry looked around nervously. "I've got to go. Frankie gave me a strict time limit."

"I thought you were his boss," Daffodil sneered. "Not his sidekick."

"Yeah, hold on, Dad," Charlie said. "I've got more questions."

"And I don't have the answers. Frankie is running the show now."

"So that's it?" Charlie couldn't believe his ears. "You're just buggering off?"

"And you ain't gonna tell me nothin about my past?" Daffodil spat. "Not even a hint?"

"Frankie will explain everything soon, I promise."

"I'm done with this clown." The girl turned away in disgust. "Seems like the best thing he did for you was vamoose."

"Good luck, son. I love you."

Gerry reached out a hand to switch off the link and Charlie tilted his head. On his dad's palm was a message in red pen.

Frankie is fighting his programming.
Don't trust him.

The screen went blank.

"Wait!" Charlie grabbed Daffodil. "Make him come back!"

"Got no idea how." She gave the computer a listless pat. "Was that jerk for real? Are the two of us supposed to take on some giant evil corporation on our lonesome?"

"Jeez," Charlie groaned. "My dad's a criminal on the run and wants me to follow the instructions of some glorified laptop." He gritted his teeth. "I can't do it. I'm just a kid."

"Aw, if you were any more cautious you'd have your own shell." Daffodil tapped her neck. "I say we talk to Frankie. I got a few choice words for him and most of them ain't printable."

"Don't you dare!"

"You gotta be wondering what he wants us to do," she said. "Or why your dad sounded like Frankie was in charge of him and not the other way round."

"No." Charlie flopped face down onto his bed. "No, I'm not. I just want this to go away. I want *you* to go away."

"So what are these extraordinary abilities Frankie thinks you have?" Daffodil plopped down next to him. "Can you fly? Breathe underwater? Run at super speed?" She nudged him conspiratorially. "You got a cape? Or do ya just wear underpants on top of your jeans?"

"I don't have any special abilities!" Charlie put the pillow over his head. "I'm completely average in every way."

"Yeah, yeah. And you *always* come in fifth at sports." The girl wasn't put off. "Sounds like you do it on purpose."

"You're a moron. Now sod off."

"Frankie has us both over a barrel, my friend." Daffodil jerked the pillow away and pulled him to his feet. "And your dad, too, from what I heard. But I see how much you miss him and how protective you are of your mom. No matter how crazy this story seems, you won't ignore it, in case he's telling the truth."

"How can you act so chirpy after what you just heard?"

"'Cause, if I didn't, I'd be like you."

She opened the window and peered into the darkness. Somewhere, a dog began barking.

"Anyhow, I reckon I'll never find out who I am unless I play ball." She hooked one leg over the sill. "Now kiss me."

"What?" Charlie spluttered. "I don't even like you."

"Charming." Daffodil grasped the drainpipe beside the window. "If someone from Manticorps *is* watching the house, it'll look like you're sneakin your girlfriend out late at night, just like your paw said. Even average guys do that. Though you seem dead set on being *below* average."

Before the boy could protest, she grabbed his head and pressed her lips against his. They were soft and tasted of prawn cocktail crisps.

"Not bad." She let go and winked. "See you later, alligator." She pointed to his hand. "And take those splinters out before they go septic. Splinters you obviously can't *feel*."

Then she slid down the drainpipe and into darkness.

Three gardens away, a balding man lowered his night-vision goggles.

"Looks like Charlie's finally pulled, Victor," he said. "Didn't think he had it in him. That sad sack's not the most sociable type."

"Doesn't explain why our listening devices have suddenly stopped working," his companion replied. "I'm calling it in."

"Don't go off the deep end, boss. Manticorps will send a fake council worker round in a couple of days to plant new ones. Then we can waste another month listening to that boring kid ignoring his mum while she talks about The X Factor." He put his night-vision goggles away. "If those two know anything about Gerry Ray's whereabouts, I'm the Queen of Sheba."

"I don't agree," Victor said. "A midnight visitor and all our surveillance equipment suddenly going dark is too much of a coincidence. The vice president will want to know."

"Rather you than me. That woman is terrifying. Even fire couldn't kill her."

"Comes with the territory." Victor rose up from behind the bush where he had been hiding. He was frighteningly large, with a scar running round his throat like a noose. "It's high time we took that family in for some proper questioning."

Charlie tossed and turned fitfully. At 7.00 a.m. he got up, dressed and checked on his mum. She was snoring quietly so he went for a walk to clear his head.

The winter sun was creeping over the rooftops, dripping light between the chimney pots, and the streets of his quiet neighbourhood were almost deserted. It suddenly struck Charlie that Daffodil couldn't have had anywhere to go. He might dislike her, but the fact that she had probably spent the night in some bitterly cold doorway made him feel even worse.

He bought a sandwich at the corner shop and sat on a park bench at the end of his lane, lost in melancholy.

Last night had to be some kind of elaborate hoax. *Had* to be.

But his father wouldn't pull such a cruel stunt. He must be telling the truth.

Besides, things that had never made sense before seemed to fit into this dreadful new scenario. The fact that Gerry had vanished without saying goodbye. That he'd left them with no money. The way his mum had become withdrawn and jumpy, unwilling to let Charlie out of her sight. He had thought it was because she was depressed and lonely. Now he could see a different reason.

She was *afraid*.

Suddenly his dreary street seemed an altogether more sinister place. The twitching curtains at number 10. The old guy from number 12, always out clipping his hedge, whether it needed trimming or not. The big green van with 'Gregory's Plumbing' on the side, parked a few doors down.

The sandwich stopped on its way to Charlie's lips.

He had never paid the vehicle much attention because it was always there. Now he wondered what kind of plumber didn't ever get called out on a job.

The boy breathed deeply and evenly, trying to calm himself. It was no good. His parents had lied about their past and his dad was on the run. His house was being watched by a sinister corporation. And a dangerous entity that created weapons and killed people wanted him to team up with some nutty girl and act like an action hero.

He felt like a volcano threatening to erupt.

"Just keep calm," he murmured to himself. "Think of kittens or something."

But he couldn't. Lately, it seemed his mind worked in a different way. Logically. Methodically.

And something else was bothering him.

His father's story didn't ring true.

Gerry and his mum had given up their computer-hacking crusade so he could have a normal life. That sounded like the decent, loving parents he knew. So why would his father throw it all away by breaking into the Marginal Science Division? If he was that good, surely he could have downloaded Frankie remotely and wiped Manticorps' data without setting foot in the place. It didn't make sense.

Cogs and gears shifted in the boy's head.

"Hang on."

His chest tightened as everything fell into place.

"I know what you were really after, Dad. And it *wasn't* Frankie."

He straightened up and ran a hand through his hair, smoothing it down. Now another ordeal awaited him.

He had to confront his mother and find out exactly what she knew.

When he let himself into the house, Daffodil McNugget was sitting in the kitchen with his mum, both laughing and sipping steaming mugs of coffee.

"There you are!" His mother looked relieved. "Never known you to be up before one o' clock during the holidays." She stretched and yawned. "Me? I've just had the best sleep in ages."

"That's... eh... good." Charlie glared at Daffodil. She had dark circles under her eyes but, apart from that, seemed as irritatingly chirpy as the night before.

"Your friend Daffodil here came round to visit, but you were out." His mum got up and gave her son a hug. "So we've been having a nice chat and I'm making a spot of brunch." She indicated a large pan of bacon and eggs sizzling on the stove. "Daff says she recently moved to Scotland and you've been showing her around. That is *so* nice."

I am going to kill you! Charlie mouthed over his mother's shoulder, fighting down his ire. Daffodil merely grinned and blew him a kiss.

"I came to see if you'd like to check out the science exhibition at the museum with me," she said. "Suddenly I have quite a fascination with technology."

"I'm busy," he replied brusquely, clenching both fists behind his back.

"Chuckles!" His mum let go, cheeks scarlet. "Don't be so rude." She sat back down and patted Daffodil's shoulder. "He must have got out of the wrong side of the bed this morning."

"You call him *Chuckles*?" Daffodil stifled a smirk.

"Oh, he used to be a happy wee soul," Marion replied regretfully. "Before he turned into a teenager."

"*Mum!*"

"That's OK, Mrs Ray." The girl slurped her coffee loudly. "I don't want to *bug* him."

"Please call me Marion. Mrs Ray sounds so… old."

"And you can call me Mac," the girl replied. "Daffodil seems a bit… formal. Pretentious even."

"Idiotic, more like," Charlie mumbled under his breath. Still, the girl was obviously picking up a fine vocabulary from Frankie.

The doorbell rang.

"My goodness, what an eventful morning." Marion got to her feet again and went to answer the door. "We even had a power cut earlier, though it's back on now."

Charlie rounded on Daffodil as soon as his mother was out of earshot.

"What the hell are you playing at? I told you I didn't want—"

"Power cut, huh?" She silenced him with a wave of her hand. "You see any other houses affected while you were out? 'Cause I sure didn't."

"No," he confessed.

"Gimme your phone." Daffodil held out her hand. "Quick."

Puzzled, Charlie handed it over.

His mum came back in, followed by a balding man wearing blue overalls.

"Hi folks," he said pleasantly. "I'm here to check your circuits. Had a few calls this morning about a disruption to the electrical grid in the area."

"That was fast." Marion picked up the kettle and filled it. "No offence, but you really don't expect prompt service these days. Would you like a coffee?"

"None taken. And I'd love a brew." He hoisted a leather tool belt higher on his waist. "If you'll show me where the fuse box is, it won't take a minute to check."

"What a coincidence!" Daffodil had the phone pressed against her ear. "I'm just talkin to my dad and he works for the power company too."

"Really?" The man looked uncomfortable.

Charlie glanced at his companion. The phone was switched off, but the girl's other hand was resting on her neck, touching the bulge where Frankie's chip was implanted. He knew exactly who was talking to her.

"Dad's askin if you checked the signal box on Marchmont Road," she said. "The one between Tesco and the bettin office?"

"First thing I tried." The man relaxed. "But it seems to be fine, so now I'm going house to house."

"Really?" Daffodil tossed the mobile back to Charlie, who caught it without looking. "'Cause I just made that whole spiel up."

"Eh... Must be crossed wires, love." The man laughed nervously, turning to Marion. "Crossed wires, get it? Now, if you'll show me the fuse box, madam." He reached into a large pouch on the side of his belt.

Marion swung the kettle and it connected with the stranger's stubbled jaw. The blow lifted the man off the ground and he landed on the Formica counter with a horrific thud. Charlie skipped back as an automatic pistol dropped from the tool belt and clattered across the floor.

The man sat up, shaking his head. Marion slammed her kettle into his face and he crashed back down, sliding along the counter until his head dropped into the sink.

"Charles Ray." She blew a wisp of hair from her face. "I think you owe me an explanation."

"I owe *you* an explanation?" The boy's eyes were like saucers. "When did my mum turn into Jackie Chan?"

"Not now, Chaz." Daffodil still had one hand on her neck and it was obvious Frankie was continuing to relay information to her. "The most likely strategy for our abduction is to have one member of a four-man team infiltrate the buildin disguised as a tradesman, so as not to alert the neighbours. Two more will sneak through the gardens and force the back door. The last person will be hidden out front in case we make a run for it."

"We'll discuss this situation later, Mac, including how the hell you know all that."

Marion grabbed a carving knife from the rack beside her as a heavily armed assailant flung himself through the kitchen window in a halo of shattered glass. Before the intruder could raise his rifle, Charlie's mum buried the blade in his hand. He dropped the weapon with a screech of pain. Marion butted the astonished man in the face and finished him off with another wallop of her kettle.

"I know how to handle myself," she informed Daffodil.

"You do seem to have everythin covered, Mrs R." Daffodil slid off her seat and under the table. "I'll get outta your way."

The door to the back garden burst open and slammed into Marion. She sprawled across the floor, clutching her head.

Silhouetted in the frame was the largest man Charlie had ever seen. He had an ugly scar running round his throat like a noose. And he held an automatic pistol in each hand.

"Up against the wall," he barked. "All of you,"

"You hurt my mum." Charlie's eyes narrowed.

"Oh dear," Daffodil chirped from under the table. "Bad move, King Kong."

"Against the wall, kid." Victor motioned with the pistols. "Pronto."

"*Nobody* messes with my mother." Charlie walked towards him.

"Don't be a moron," the giant growled. "I *will* shoot you."

Charlie somersaulted sideways onto the kitchen table, landing on splayed hands. He bent his elbows, arched his back and pushed as Victor fired. Bullets gouged furrows in the wood, but the boy was already in the air. Both of his feet crashed down on the handle of the frying pan. Bacon, eggs and hot fat sailed across the room and hit the giant square in his face. He gave a high-pitched scream and clawed at his eyes. Charlie caught the pan effortlessly in mid-flight, spun with the precision of a discus thrower and hurled it like a Frisbee. The pan crunched into the man's forehead, knocking him backwards into the garden. As Victor attempted to get up, Charlie followed him outside, picking up the discarded pan as he went.

Thunk. Thunk. Thunk.

Daffodil covered her ears.

"I didn't kill him." Charlie strode back in. "Wanted to, but didn't." He helped his mother to her feet. "You all right, Mum?"

"I'll survive." Marion winced, feeling a bruise rising on her temple. "But we need to have a serious talk when this is over, young man."

"That's exactly what *I* was going to say."

"There's probably one more goon out front." Daffodil emerged from cover. "Pity you don't have any special *abilities*, Chaz."

"Not the time." The boy checked his garden for any more intruders. "This way."

"I am *not* sneaking out the back door of my own damned house." Marion put both hands on her hips. "Besides, we need transportation."

"We haven't got a car any more, Mum."

"I'm taking the green van that's kept us under surveillance for the last few weeks." She unfastened her apron. "And woe betide anyone who gets in my way."

"So you *did* know we were being watched?"

"We've both been hiding things from each other, and it was a mistake." Marion pushed the pair into the hall. "But all that will have to wait."

"That woman's a devil in a dress!" Daffodil punched Charlie on the arm. "Chaz, I *really* like your mom."

The trio stopped at the front door.

"Likely position of the last man?" Daffodil held her neck.

"Why is Mac talking to herself?" Marion asked.

"Long story." Charlie cocked the rifle he had picked up from the kitchen floor. "But we need her. For now."

"Ahem." His mother pointed at the weapon. "Don't even *think* of using that."

"Mum, we're fighting for our lives."

"You *know* how I feel about guns, Charlie Ray." Marion snatched the rifle from him. "I'm well aware of your capabilities, so find another way."

"You *are*?"

"Think I haven't noticed you changing?" she replied sharply. "I just didn't know what to do about it. Now put down the gun."

"All right," Charlie sighed. "Back in a minute." He trudged up the stairs, muttering to himself, and plodded back down a few seconds later holding his bat and baseball. "Ready."

"What's *that* for, slugger?" Daffodil goggled. "You gonna challenge the goon out front to a game of catch?"

"You do your thing and I'll do mine."

"If you insist." Daffodil peered through the letterbox at the van.

"There are a lot of nosy neighbours here who'd report any suspicious activity to the police, so the last guy is probably hidden in the cab of that surveillance vehicle. With a sniper rifle."

"How do we get him out?"

"He has limited sightlines in there. Can't hit two targets if they're headin in opposite directions." Daffodil winked at Charlie's mum. "Mrs R? You willin to stake your life on Chaz bein as good as you think?"

"Of course, Mac. He's my boy."

"Then let's go."

Before Charlie could stop them, Daffodil and Marion flung open the door and raced down the path. When they reached the gate, Daffodil went left and Charlie's mum turned right, both sprinting as fast as they could.

A black-clad figure wearing a balaclava leapt from the driver's side of the van. He knelt and raised a rifle to his cheek, aiming at Marion's back.

"Hey, woolhead!" Charlie threw the baseball up in the air. "Picked the wrong target!"

The assassin glanced round as the boy swung his bat. It hit the descending ball with a loud crack and the missile whizzed through the air, thudding into the man's temple. He dropped the gun, tumbled over and lay still.

"Strike one!" Daffodil came sprinting back. "C'mon, Mrs R."

They climbed into the cab of the green van and Charlie's mum rolled down the window. Their neighbour from number 12 was peering over the hedge, trimming shears motionless in his hands.

"Morning, Mr Cuthbertson!" Marion gave a friendly wave. "Can you do me a favour and cancel my milk and paper deliveries?"

"No problem, hen." The man's eyes darted towards the

unconscious figure lying in the middle of the road. "Ehm... I take it you won't be coming back any time soon."

"I don't imagine so."

"You were always quick with a smile or a chat." He gave a small salute. "If anyone asks, I'll say you went the other way."

"You're a proper gentleman." She gunned the engine into life and drove off.

"So where are we going?" Marion asked Daffodil. "You seem to have all the answers, young lady."

"I was sent from a place near some village called Bellbowrie," she replied. "Apparently it was Gerry Ray's safe house."

"Gerry?" Charlie's mother whirled round. "You *know* my husband?"

"Eyes front, Mum. You almost hit a lamppost."

"Has he contacted you, Mac? What's going on?"

"He got in touch last night," Charlie admitted. "Said he loved us and he was in trouble."

"That I already knew." Marion swerved back onto the road. "But I can't just drive to Bellbowrie. A van with all this surveillance equipment must have some kind of tracer system. Saw it on *CSI Miami.*"

Daffodil put her hand on the dashboard and wisps of smoke began to rise from behind the plastic vent. "Not any more it don't."

"Impressive." Marion waved the grey tendrils away. "Now, do you pair of delinquents want to tell me exactly what Gerry had to say for himself?"

Marion's phone rang.

"I'll put it on silent." The woman pulled her mobile out with one hand and checked who was calling. The screen said:

Charlie saw Marion blanch when she read the name. She really *had* known what his dad was up to.

"You better get that," Daffodil advised. "It'll be important."

Charlie's mum pulled over, pressed receive and held the phone to her ear. She listened for a few minutes, then lowered the device.

"Carry on without me," she said quietly.

"You can't go back to the house," Charlie argued. "Not after what happened."

"I won't. But I'm getting out here."

"What did Frankie say?" he demanded. "Did he *threaten* you?"

"He told me how to find your dad but gave me a job to do first."

"What did he *say?*"

"I have to get out now, baby." Marion's mouth was pinched into a thin line. "He promised to keep you safe, though. He *better.*" She pulled her son close and kissed his forehead. "I have faith in you. And I love you with all my heart."

"I love you too, Mum."

"Mac?" Marion let Charlie go. "You'll look after my boy, won't you?"

"Don't worry, Mrs R." Daffodil crossed her heart. "I ain't gonna let Chaz out of my sight."

"That's the last thing I want to hear," Charlie groaned. "Can't you just tell me—?"

"Not now, baby." Marion cut him off. "Do you know how to drive?"

"I've never sat behind a wheel in my life."

"Not what I asked. You've been watching me do it for five minutes."

"Yes," he said dejectedly. "I know how to drive."

"When we were young, your dad and I wanted to make the world a better place. Took some crazy risks to do it." His mum put two fingers to her lips and pressed them against Charlie's cheek. "I'm afraid it's your turn. On you go. Be brave."

Marion got out of the van and waved miserably as it drove away. Then she waited in the middle of the road, watching sunlight filtering through the leaves above. She shook her hands and breathed out slowly, as if preparing for an innocent jog.

Another van crested the rise and came tearing towards her at breakneck speed, just as Frankie had predicted it would.

Manticorps had had *two* surveillance vans watching the house.

Marion pulled out the pistol she had grabbed, unobserved, from the kitchen floor. Standing her ground, she emptied the clip into the oncoming vehicle's tyres.

The van veered to the right, missing her by inches. It clipped a tree, ploughed through the undergrowth and bounced across a field, steam pouring from the engine.

"I thought we'd put this life behind us, Gerry." Marion wiped the weapon clean and dropped it on the asphalt. "Never dreamed we'd pass it on to our son."

Then she drifted away, quiet as a ghost.

Charlie drove in silence, out of the city and into the countryside, Daffodil giving directions.

"Turn left here," she said, as they approached their destination.

He pulled into a secluded driveway. The safe house was a modern two-storey building hidden behind a high wall and overlooking a large garden. In one corner was a huge oak with a tree house built into its upper branches. A makeshift swing consisting of a rope and tyre dangled from one thick bough. At the bottom, separated by a wire fence, was a field containing a parked tractor.

They drove into an adjoining garage and pulled down the corrugated iron door. The house was unlocked and keys hung from a hook in the hall.

Gerry Ray was gone.

The pair trooped into a spacious living room, furnished with expensive leather couches. On one wall was a map of Edinburgh. A huge PC sat on a desk beside open French windows, curtains billowing in the breeze. Outside was a wooden balcony with a view across the Pentland Hills.

"Fancy, ain't it?" Daffodil said admiringly. "Your dad must be richer than a gold-plated chocolate cake to afford such a swell pad."

"I'm pretty sure Frankie supplied the funds." Charlie went looking for the kitchen. "I'm going to make some tea and then we'll talk."

"No sugar for me, Chaz. I'm sweet enough."

"Make your own damned tea. Can't you get it into your head that we're not friends?"

"I'll just have coffee then."

Charlie stormed out of the room, leaving Daffodil sitting on the wide chesterfield couch. But he came back with two cups on the tray.

"Cheers." She accepted the brew. "Hospitality is the cornerstone of civilisation, as Grandma used to say."

"You remember your *grandmother*?"

"Nah. I was just making conversation."

"Can't you be serious for one sodding minute?" Charlie sank onto the couch beside her. "Doesn't the situation we're in even bother you?"

"That's why I'm trying to lighten the mood, dummy." Daffodil sipped her drink. "But I'm happy to stop jokin if you'll start comin clean."

"How do you mean?"

"Look." She grabbed his hands and turned them over so the palms were showing. "Last night these were cut to ribbons. Now you're completely healed."

"They were just some splinters."

"You also beat up an armed intruder who looked like a shaved gorilla." The girl wasn't put off. "Wanna tell me how you managed that?"

"No."

"You really need to work on your communication skills, Chaz."

"I mean I don't want to talk about it. And stop calling me Chaz."

"You got nobody left to confide in, bub." Daffodil swivelled round in her seat until she was looking him in the eye. "So how about pullin that grouchy head out of your butt for five minutes, huh? What are you hidin?"

Charlie stared at the floor for a while. When he looked up, his eyes were red-rimmed.

"I've always been sickly. Had severe bouts of meningitis ever since I was a baby."

Daffodil touched her neck. Charlie guessed Frankie was informing her that meningitis was a life-threatening viral infection.

"Oof," she said. "Sounds pretty bad."

"A month ago I had another attack. One that turned into pneumonia. I was hospitalised and my parents thought I was going to die." His voice was flat. "I was sure it was why my dad left. Because he couldn't deal with me any more."

"I can understand his point."

"Mac. If I'm going to make the effort…"

"Sorry, force of habit. Go on."

"Then, suddenly, I was fine." Charlie's hands trembled and he almost spilled his drink. "The doctors had never seen anything like it. What's more, I haven't had a day's illness since."

"That's good, ain't it?"

"I'm not just fine." He blew on his tea. "I'm… different."

"Howd'ya mean?"

"It's going to sound weird."

"You don't say?" Daffodil feigned surprise. "And I been havin such a normal couple of days."

"I'm faster and stronger than I used to be." Charlie flexed his muscles. "What's more, I can perform Olympic-level gymnastics or black-belt kung fu or play guitar like a rock star, just by watching someone do it on TV. I could manage that van after five minutes of looking at my mother drive." He seemed lost for a second. "I didn't tell Mum about my abilities 'cause I was scared. But I guess she spotted it anyway." He shook his head sadly. "She obviously knew a lot more than she was letting on."

"Handy talent to have, instant expertise." Daffodil was suitably impressed. "No wonder Frankie picked you."

"I ain't convinced that's the reason." Charlie's voice was suddenly huskier and his accent took on a weird twang. "I'm five foot five and weigh eighty pounds. Hardly the type to save the world, huh?"

"Holy cow!" Daffodil's jaw dropped. "You sound *exactly* like me."

"Told you." His tone returned to normal. "There's nothing I can't copy."

"You got any idea how it happened?"

"Didn't have a clue until I talked to Dad."

"Ole hairy-face didn't say anything about that. I was listenin."

"Worked it out myself," Charlie said flatly. "Right after he broke into Manticorps' Marginal Research Division, I miraculously began to recover. All signs of meningitis and pneumonia gone." He closed his eyes. "My father didn't infiltrate Manticorps to free Frankie. He went to steal the Atlas Serum."

"The stuff that makes soldiers faster and stronger?"

"And resistant to disease." Charlie sipped his tea. "He sacrificed his own freedom in the hope that some experimental drug would give me the strength to survive."

"No kiddin!"

"He probably went straight to the hospital after he escaped from Manticorps' labs and made me drink it. I was so delirious, I wouldn't even have known he was there."

"Seems like it worked. And your pop's a regular hero, to boot." Daffodil looked bewildered. "So why ain't you happier?"

"You heard him. The Atlas Serum wasn't only designed to make soldiers stronger and smarter. It made them more aggressive too. And we're talking about trained, disciplined men, not a short-arsed teenager." Charlie studied his hands but there wasn't a mark on them. "Whatever is running through my veins is *changing* me. And for the worse."

"You talkin about sproutin hair and extra teeth?" The girl shuffled back and held up her hands. "Do I need to fetch a rolled-up newspaper?"

"Who knows? I'm trying to control my new abilities, but I don't know if I can." Charlie rapped white knuckles against his head. "I'm always angry these days. Can't remember the last time I smiled."

"You're a teenager," Daffodil said sympathetically. "I doubt anyone will notice."

"I don't think the way I used to either. My mind makes leaps of logic it wasn't capable of before."

"That so? Gimme an example."

"OK." Charlie pointed to the computer. "If Dad wanted to talk to me last night, Frankie could have accessed my PC from right here in this room."

"What about Manticorps' bugs?"

"A running tap or radio hiss will disrupt any listening device." Charlie spread his hands. "Why go to all the trouble of sending you?"

"Maybe he thought I should get out more. I'm kinda lackin in the life-experience department."

"I think Frankie knew a set of short-circuited devices and a strange girl climbing my drainpipe would force Manticorps into action," Charlie said glumly. "Their goons would move in and I'd have to go on the run. It was his way of *guaranteeing* I'd end up here." The boy's lip curled in revulsion. "Now I've got no choice but to fight back if my family is ever going to be safe."

"That's pretty sneaky." Daffodil pouted. "I'm gettin awful tired of bein used, Chaz. Or maybe I'm just tired. I haven't slept for almost two days now." She yawned loudly. "There's only one way we can find out what's really goin on. We gotta talk to Frankie."

"I suppose we'd better." Charlie nodded. "I've got plenty of questions and, like you, most of them contain a swear word or two."

"So go ahead and ask him." She indicated the PC. "He can access any computer and appear on its screen."

"So you don't need to touch it?"

"That was just to get your attention. I'm a bit of a show-off sometimes."

"You don't say. But I want you to leave the room."

"Why?"

"It's a private conversation."

Daffodil looked hurt but tapped her neck anyway. "Frankie would prefer me to stay. He says we're a team."

"I don't care what he'd prefer," Charlie persisted. "If he wants my help, you'll both have to suck it up."

"I'm part of this too, Chaz. Why are you being so bloody-minded?"

"I'll make it quick," he relented. "I promise."

"All right," Daffodil moped. "You make rotten coffee anyway. I'm going to get my own."

She marched out of the room.

"What part of 'we're a team' did you not get?" The computer sprang to life, a swarm of coloured dots appearing on the screen. "This isn't a great start to our relationship."

The voice had a synthetic timbre but was far more animated than the boy had anticipated.

"You don't talk the way I thought you would." Charlie blinked in surprise.

"What? You were expecting a Dalek?"

"Something like that, yes."

"I've been picking up my vocabulary from YouTube, so I can blend in. Still don't get the point of Grumpy Cat, though. I mean, he can't help the way he looks. What's so funny about that?" Frankie sniggered in a disturbingly human way. "He does look at bit like you, though."

"Quite finished?" The boy was determined not to be wrong-footed.

"Not in the slightest. But you'd better cut to the chase before Daffodil starts listening at the door. She's getting fed up of following instructions."

"You too, apparently."

Gerry's warning flashed into Charlie's mind again.

Frankie is fighting his programming.

"I sense a certain hostility towards myself and Mac. Have you considered therapy?"

"Have you considered shutting up for a second?" the boy replied evenly. "This conversation isn't something she needs to hear, all right?"

"Oh sure. Why include the only pal you've got? You've got some serious trust issues, kid."

"Where are my mum and dad, Frankie? Are they all right?"

"Gerry is alive and safe, and Marion is on her way to join him. But don't bother calling her. I jammed her phone."

"I need proof."

"Like their exact locations? Why don't I draw a map, tell you which bus goes there and wave goodbye from the front door? Actually, forget the last bit. I don't have hands."

"Why didn't Dad wait here for me?" Charlie refused to rise to the bait.

"A father-and-son reunion? That's the kind of distraction I don't need."

"It's not up to you!"

"Here's the deal, pal," Frankie said slowly. "You do what I say without asking any more questions. In return, I'll see you're all reunited when this is over. I'll also tell Daffodil who she really is and how to remove my chip from her neck. Sound fair?"

"Sounds like blackmail." The boy's eye twitched.

"Gerry Ray programmed me to protect human life. That includes you, Mac, and your parents, whether I like the idea or not." Frankie made a sniffing noise. "He didn't say I had to be nice about it."

In the kitchen, they could hear Daffodil stirring her coffee.

"The point is, you'll never be safe until the threat from Manticorps is neutralised, and that's exactly what you're going to help me do. I'm not offering you a choice, so stop acting like some spoiled brat."

Charlie tried to stay calm, but he could feel hot rage bubbling up inside him. "I should believe the word of some machine?"

"I'm NOT a machine. I'm an artificial intelligence. At least your father knew the difference."

"I'm not my father." Charlie pulled a knife he had taken from the kitchen out of his belt and held it up. "The Atlas Serum has made me *very* unpredictable."

"If by 'unpredictable' you mean 'crazy as a box of frogs', I couldn't agree more. I'm not actually in this computer, so what do you hope to achieve with that?"

"Just checking you can see me." He nodded at the screen's tiny camera.

"I can. Congratulations. You win a lollipop."

"Now I'll make *you* a promise," the boy said icily. "If I suspect for one moment you're lying about my parents being all right, I will cut you out of Daffodil's neck and drop your chip down the nearest drain."

"Nice try. But removing me in such a crude manner would seriously hurt your friend."

"I don't *have* any friends." Charlie's eyes glittered. "Better remember that." He threw the knife across the room. It hit bull's-eye on a tatty dartboard attached to the wall.

"That was certainly to the point." Frankie laughed uproariously. "Get it? I made a joke."

"I don't have a sense of humour." The boy stepped back, breathing heavily. "And you'd better keep this conversation to yourself."

"Look. We seem to have got off on the wrong foot." Frankie sounded contrite. "I'm just a bit annoyed. Programmed to do this and that and given no choice about it. In a way, we're in the same boat."

"With you as the captain. Meanwhile Mac and I are going to be doing the rowing without knowing where we're going."

"Nice analogy." Frankie chuckled. "It all rhymed too. When this is done, maybe you can write an epic poem about our adventures."

"You trying to get on my good side? 'Cause I haven't got one of those either."

"How about this as a peace offering, then? Gerry Ray stuck a letter addressed to you in the top drawer of the dresser, when he thought I wasn't looking. I'm dying to know the contents but I didn't ask Daffodil to read it to me and I won't ever pester you about what it says. That's how trust works. See where I'm going with this?"

"Spare me the lecture." Charlie glowered. "And I still don't know why you picked a fourteen year old to help you, even if I do have a few talents."

"'Cause you've got a winning personality and nice teeth. No more whining. I hold all the cards and you know it."

"You can come back now, Mac," the boy shouted angrily.

"In a minute. Got my hand stuck in the espresso machine."

"I'm afraid she's a bit clueless without me."

"We'll see about that. And switch off that damned camera. I've been spied on enough by Manticorps."

"Have a nap, then. You were up half the night and lack of shut-eye is making you crabby."

"I don't need much sleep these days. This is just the way I am."

"But Daffodil does. She must be on her last legs, and no amount of coffee will fix that."

The light on the computer went out and the girl sauntered back in, two fingers stuck in her mouth. She seemed rather unsteady on her feet.

"Find out anything interestin?" She rubbed her eyes and yawned again.

"Nope," Charlie sighed. "I only had time for a short chat."

Daffodil turned her head and gave a sharp intake of breath. "Why is there a knife stickin out of that round thing?" She tilted her head as Frankie fed her more information. "Oh. It's a dartboard. You were playin a game?"

"Sort of. I lost."

Charlie walked over to the dartboard, pulled out the knife and yanked open the dresser drawer. He removed an envelope and used the blade to open it.

There was one page, written in his father's neat handwriting.

Son.

You must memorise the string of numbers on the other side of the paper, then destroy it. If this message does fall into the wrong hands, the sequence will be meaningless to most people. But you are not most people and I'm sure you will figure it out. It might come in useful as a bargaining chip.

But whatever you do, don't EVER let Frankie see it.

I love you, kid.
Dad

Charlie flipped the scrap of paper over. On the other side was a string of numbers.

55 45 86 962 04 334 145 223 52972

"We better memorise this." Daffodil leaned over his shoulder.

"No need." Charlie tore up the page before she could see it properly. "I've done it."

"Jeezy peeps." The girl looked stunned. "Bet *you* don't need to make a list when you go shoppin." She staggered a little and leaned against the wall to right herself. "Chaz, I don't feel so good. I'm *really* tired."

"Go sit down then." He pushed her away. "I'm trying to work out what this sequence *means*."

He closed his eyes and concentrated. Gerry thought he could

interpret what the numbers meant and so he'd try his hardest. Maybe it was a cipher. Or coordinates of some sort.

There was a thump behind him.

When Charlie turned round, his companion was lying on the floor.

Daffodil woke under the duvet of an enormous bed in a pink and white room. The curtains were open and birds twittered outside. She stretched and rolled over.

"What the…?"

Charlie was sitting in an armchair watching her. On the bedside table was a tray, laden with coffee, muffins and toast.

"You don't half snore," he said.

"And you got the manners of a junkyard dog in a bone factory." Daffodil looked around suspiciously. "How did I get here?"

"I carried you." The boy handed her a slice of toast. "You've been out cold since yesterday afternoon."

The girl peered under her covers.

"Chill out," Charlie said. "You're still wearing your clothes. But if you want to get changed, the wardrobe is full of stuff your size." He bit into a muffin. "Mine too. Frankie seems to have thought of everything."

"That's a mixed blessing." Daffodil rolled her eyes. He ain't got much fashion sense, if my last outfit was anything to go by."

She propped herself up on the pillow and took a slurp of coffee.

"So, you ready to have another go at findin out what Frankie actually wants us to do?"

"I bet you've already tried that, despite me asking you not to."

"Course I did. But he won't tell me nothin unless you're in on the conversation."

"All right. Just don't expect me to be nice about it."

"There's a surprise. We'll use the computer in the living room."

"Get up then." Charlie patted his knees. "Grab a shower and let's chat with our boss."

"Eh... Chaz?" Daffodil drummed on the covers.

"What?"

"I'm awful cute, but you gotta understand that that kiss we shared was just for show. I sure as hell ain't gettin undressed in front of you."

"Sorry! Sorry!" He backed out of the door, cheeks scarlet.

A slow grin spread over Daffodil's face.

"I don't think you're as bad as you make out, Mr Unsociable."

Charlie was wearing the same outfit he'd had on yesterday. The boy had obviously sat by her bedside all night.

Daffodil finally emerged from the bedroom, combing her damp hair. She was wearing a yellow polka dot dress and pink cardigan.

'Yikes!" Charlie was on the couch, finishing off his own breakfast.

"Soon as we get the chance, bub, I'm goin clothes shoppin."

"I'll drive you. That outfit's making my eyes hurt."

"Moment of truth, Chaz." She snapped her fingers. "Talk to us, Frankie."

The computer flickered to life. A pattern of glowing orbs appeared on the screen and the red light of the camera began to glow again.

"The boy wonder is here," Daffodil proclaimed. "And ready to participate. You wanna give us the low-down?"

"Have a nice sleep, Charlie?" the computer asked, as if nothing had happened the day before. "Or did you spend half the night fuming about your situation?"

"What do you think?"

There was a yawning noise from the screen. "And... that's the sound of me not giving a damn."

"Y'all must have had an interestin conversation." Daffodil raised an eyebrow. "I don't think Frankie cares for you much, Chazzle."

"Aw, I like the kid fine. I'm just trying to get a bit of banter going."

"Start with something simpler," she suggested. "Like getting him to smile."

"I'm waiting for one of you to actually say something funny," Charlie grunted.

"That's more like it!"

"I'm sure Chaz has plenty of questions." Daffodil relaxed on the couch and put both hands behind her head. "I'll join in whenever I got somethin irrelevant to say."

"My first is a no-brainer." Charlie didn't bother with niceties. "What the hell are you? You seem light years ahead of any AI I ever read about."

"Me too," Daffodil added. "And I don't just read comic books."

"Manticorps kind of invented me by mistake. Those idiots didn't even realise what they'd stumbled across at first." The screen showed a clip of clowns chasing each other round a circus ring.

"Some hotshot analyst in the Marginal Science Department wrote a programme amalgamating the billions of algorithms already existing on the web. Thought it would be a useful predictive tool. Instead, he produced an artificial intelligence, far smarter than any human. That would be yours truly."

"No need to big yourself up," Daffodil rolled her eyes. "We all know what a smarty-pants you are."

"As soon as they realised the abilities I had, Manticorp's scientists programmed me to obey their commands and put me to work improving their projects."

"Until my dad hacked in and reprogrammed you to be the good guy."

"A bit simplistic, but close enough."

"So why the insistence on destroying Manticorps?" Charlie carried on, undeterred. "With your resources, can't you just spirit my family and Daffodil away? I wouldn't mind my own beach."

"That's a fair question."

"How about an answer?"

"'Cause I'm supposed to defend all human life, if I can."

"So? Manticorps isn't after anyone but us."

"True. Thing is, I can sift through an almost infinite amount of information on the web instantly. Calculate the most probable outcome of any set of events."

"Good for you. Maybe you can help us win the lottery."

"I'm afraid we're playing for far higher stakes than that."

Frankie paused dramatically.

"You see, I've identified a likely occurrence in the near future which will cause the end of the world."

"Say what now?" Charlie went white.

"That's a bit of a surprise, Frankie." Daffodil looked equally uneasy. "A pretty nasty one too."

"Bummer, eh? What's more, this extinction event is one that Manticorps will inadvertently trigger – which is the real reason you two are going to help me destroy them."

"Are you sure about this?" Charlie frowned. "After all, nobody can predict the future."

"No, they can't. But I'm able to assemble data from every computer system, security camera and hidden corner of the internet on this planet. Then my billions of complex algorithms calculate the most likely outcomes of what I see. And I predict Manticorps are going to cause a catastrophe."

"What kind of catastrophe?" Daffodil asked. "A war? A tidal wave?"

"I haven't narrowed it down to specifics, though we can probably rule out tidal waves. But there's no doubt those morons are the catalyst."

"Shouldn't you recruit yourself an army then, instead of two kids?" The boy folded his arms, as he always did when he was being stubborn. "Seems like there isn't much you can't manage."

"Using too many people would interfere with my delicate computations. I'd explain why, but I haven't got a spare hundred years to teach you theoretical physics."

"You deserve a kick in *your* delicate computations for that crack." Daffodil raised a booted foot. "Except I can't reach my neck."

"Oh, you're hilarious."

"Then get to the point," the girl tisked. "You're talkin more gibberish than Donald Duck's answerin machine."

"I can give you a theoretical example of how we have to work together, if that'll help."

"Better than nothing, I suppose." Charlie sat down on the couch next to Daffodil. "Our tiny minds will try and keep up."

"All right. Suppose Manticorps developed a flying human/monkey hybrid."

"A flying human monkey?"

"Yeah. That's stupid. Let's make it a flying human/octopus hybrid. Can I continue?"

"Go ahead," Charlie sighed.

"Tomorrow they intend to let it out for a test flight. But they don't realise it has a virulent disease that will turn the whole world into zombies."

"This is a pretty dopey example," Daffodil tutted.

"I'm trying to make it fun, so you'll concentrate."

"Mentioning the extinction of mankind pretty much grabbed our attention."

"Charlie's right. The most obvious move is to hire a bunch of thugs, attack Manticorps' headquarters and exterminate this thing before it gets out. Why do you think I won't do that?"

"Because people might get killed in the process," Charlie answered. "And you can't let that happen."

"Bingo. I'm programmed not to be directly responsible for any human dying, even if my inaction means the whole world getting wiped out. Gerry was trying to do the right thing, but he didn't think it through properly."

A shudder went down the boy's spine.

Frankie is fighting his programming.

If Frankie were free to act as he wanted, he could probably destroy Manticorps without too much effort. But where would he draw the line? Would *any* human life matter to him?

Daffodil stroked her chin, oblivious to Charlie's turmoil, trying to figure a way round the problem.

"You could shut down Manticorps' defences all on your own," she said. "Turn off the power and everythin."

"Sure. But I can't actually walk into their headquarters and shoot the thing."

"I see." Charlie snapped his fingers. "You'd need someone human to sneak in and kill it. Which would be me."

"Gold star for Captain Irascible."

"How are you going to do that, Chaz?" Daffodil looked puzzled. "You can see in the dark now?"

"Actually, I can. Another side effect of the Atlas Serum."

"Wow. No wonder Frankie picked you."

"Wait a minute." Charlie hesitated. "What if this octopus man can see in the dark too? And he gets the jump on me?"

"I'll send Mac to your funeral with a nice bunch of roses."

"Hey! You're supposed to be my protector."

"Ah. But it was your plan, Chaz. If you're determined to carry it out and end up kicking the bucket, that's not my fault. It's called a loophole."

"So, you can't actually *order* anyone to attack Manticorps in case there are fatalities. You need people to work *with* you, rather than *for* you."

"You're finally getting it. That's why you have to volunteer for the job."

"Volunteer?" Charlie ground his teeth. "After everything you've done to us?"

"You'd rather Manticorps watched you forever? Or at least until they captured us all?"

"I wouldn't. But what if we *do* refuse?"

"Then the human race goes the way of the dinosaurs. Your choice. And you have to believe me when I say that you two are the best bet I have for success."

"Just me and Charlie?" Daffodil looked cynical. "I sure don't rate our chances against a private army."

"Me neither," Frankie agreed. "You'll need the help of a real professional, so I'm hoping to recruit the best."

On the computer screen, a grey boxy building with towering concrete walls appeared.

"Outside Edinburgh is Sunnyside Maximum Security Facility, which houses a notorious murderer known as the White Spider. If you agree to help, your first task is to break Spidey out and enlist him to our cause."

"You're off your rocker!" Charlie choked. "That's way too difficult!"

"Not with Frankie on our side." Daffodil tried to sound reassuring. "He'll tell us how and we'll follow his instructions."

"You're not listening, Mac," Frankie replied patiently. "Like everything else, the plan to free the White Spider must be thought up by you two."

"I still don't understand." Daffodil shook her head. "You've got a brain the size of Australia. You must be able to come up with a better strategy than us."

"Can't deny that. I can think of a dozen schemes to free this guy - but they also carry the risk that someone will get bumped off. So I can't ask you to perform any of them."

"In other words," Charlie said bitterly, "you're not willing to accept the blame."

"I'm willing enough. Just not able. Your dad saw to that."

"What would happen if you decided to grow a pair?" Daffodil asked sarcastically. "Take matters into your own hands?"

"What happens if I ask you to stop breathing, Mac?"

"That sounds like a great idea," Charlie deadpanned.

"Banter's coming along nicely, kid. Point is, I've attempted everything to override my programming. But I just... can't." Coloured dots chased each other round the screen like angry fireflies. "Believe me, I've tried."

"Calm down, buddy," Daffodil said soothingly. "We get the picture."

But Charlie frowned.

Frankie is fighting his programming.
Don't trust him.

"Don't get me wrong. I'll assist in any way I can. But, like I said, you've got to volunteer for the job and think up a plan yourself. That way, if things go wrong, I won't be directly responsible for you dying. Or anyone else for that matter."

"What's so special about this White Spider, then?" the boy asked. "A prison must be full of likely candidates."

"The Spider hates Manticorps with a passion and has some extremely... unique talents. He will be an invaluable ally in the coming fight."

"He also happens to be a homicidal manic. Think you can control *him*?"

"Wouldn't have asked you to free the guy if I didn't. And I better mention that he can't be allowed to stay on the loose. You'll have to find a way to return him to Sunnyside when it's all over."

"That'll be a walk in the park, won't it?" Charlie fumed. "Then we can go on to invent time travel, discover Atlantis and win the Nobel Prize."

"I know exactly where Atlantis is. Not hard to figure out when your intelligence is off the charts. I'm still working on time travel."

"You might have smarts, bub," Daffodil wagged a finger at the screen. "But modesty sure ain't your strong point."

"Sticks and stones, Mac." Frankie chuckled. "Don't be all day thinking about it, though. Time isn't on our side."

"Seems like nothin's on our side. Not even you."

"Tick tock, guys. Don't let humanity down."

The computer went dead.

"Sounds to me like we're between a rock and a hard place, Chaz." Daffodil rummaged through the drawers of the desk until she found a pad and pens. "Let's get started." She clicked the top of a biro and handed it over. "Penny for your thoughts?"

"I think you're an idiot," Charlie snapped. "We're talking about breaking into a prison, not the neighbour's greenhouse."

"The principle's the same."

"No it isn't," he replied despairingly. "And how about freeing a murderer?"

"He'll probably want to go, won't he?"

"I'll bet he will. Won't want to be returned to prison either. Come to think of it, there's no guarantee he'll agree to help us."

"Aw, stop acting like you got less guts than a white flag on a diet." Daffodil sighed. "When the chips are down, you come through with flyin colours."

"I won a fight, drove a van and memorised some numbers. Doesn't exactly turn me into one of the Avengers."

"You make me so mad, know that? It's like pullin teeth to get you to accept you're special."

"Mac, most of my life nobody expected *anything* from me," Charlie said forlornly. "Hell, my parents were delighted if I got better than a 'C' on my school report. Now I've suddenly graduated from saving my family to saving the world." He held out a shaking hand. "So, yeah. I'm terrified."

"What about those leaps of logic you were talkin about earlier?"

"This is more like leaping off a cliff. There's nothing logical about it."

"You got me and Frankie to help, remember?" Daffodil said

good-naturedly. "We might not like each other, but if we stick together, surely we can give it a shot?"

"What did you just say?"

"Eh? A bunch of stuff. I never listen to myself."

"You said *if we stick together*." Charlie leant over and ripped a few pages from the pad. "Look. I'm going out to the balcony for a while."

"Why? You sulk better if you have a nice view?"

"No." The boy tapped his lip thoughtfully. "But I actually have the beginnings of a crazy idea."

12

Mrs Magdalene sat behind a mahogany desk uncluttered by photographs or mementos. Her office was just as impersonal. No plants. No lamps. No mirrors. No rugs on the wooden floor. Plain shelves lined the walls, laden with neatly ordered books. A set of digital clocks showed the time regions of the world. A coat rack in one corner was bare as a winter tree.

Mrs Magdalene wasn't interested in fancy possessions or any other displays of authority. As vice president of Manticorps, she didn't need to show off how powerful she was.

At the other end of the room, Victor waited patiently, his huge frame making the chair he sat in look like a toy. His face was red and swollen and ugly purple bruises mottled his forehead.

"You've worked for me for quite some time." Mrs Magdalene's face was turned away, so he could only see her profile. "I've never had reason to reprimand you before."

"You still don't." Victor shifted in his seat, which creaked alarmingly. "There was no way for me to predict the situation we encountered."

"The *situation* being your four-man squad getting soundly beaten by a housewife and a couple of children."

"One child," Victor corrected. "The girl spent most of the fight under a table."

"That almost sounded sarcastic," Mrs Magdalene mused. "Surely you're not stupid enough to antagonise me. Not after yesterday's debacle."

"Simply stating the facts, ma'am," Victor replied. "My team are all ex-servicemen and the best at what they do. Taking those people in should have been a piece of cake. It turned out to be quite the opposite."

"Enlighten me."

"The girl rumbled us and the woman started swinging a kettle about. Yeah, she got lucky and took out a couple of my men. Even so, I would have easily prevailed." Victor touched his tender head, still bewildered by what had happened. "When Charlie joined in, that was something else entirely." He indicated the wounds on his temple. "What he did to me wasn't luck. The boy moved like he'd had years of training in unarmed combat."

"And you had no inkling that Charlie Ray was capable of such feats? Even after watching his house for a month?"

"He never did anything out of the ordinary before. Seemed a bit of a loser, to be honest."

"All your reports indicate that, yes." Mrs Magdalene slowly turned her head to look at him and Victor, tough as he was, repressed a shudder.

One half of the vice president's face resembled some fearsome school matron. The other side was much worse, puckered and twisted, the flesh hard and bubbled as melted plastic. Her lip curled up over exposed teeth in a permanent sneer, as if her cheek had been unzipped, and one eye drooped alarmingly. The disfigurement made Victor's own injuries seem like gnat bites.

"What do you know about Gerry Ray?" the woman asked.

"He's on your shortlist of people who might have destroyed the Marginal Science Division," Victor replied. "That's why you had us watching the house. In case he tried to contact his family."

"And the Atlas Serum?" Mrs Magdalene opened a file on her desk.

"It was supposed to enhance human capabilities in order to make super soldiers." Victor looked surprised. "I thought that had gone nowhere."

"We suffered a few setbacks, but an unexpected breakthrough put the project back on track." The vice president studied the papers in front of her. "After yesterday, I'd say Gerry Ray's son bears all the hallmarks of having been given just such a drug."

"He couldn't have beaten me otherwise," Victor concurred.

"I'm now utterly convinced that Gerry Ray stole our research." Mrs Magdalene stared out of the window. "Then he burned down our lab, killed our scientists and did *this* to me." She stroked her scars with the gloved hand. "Naturally, I'm very keen to find his whereabouts."

Victor stayed quiet, well aware that Mrs Magdalene wanted vengeance rather than sympathy.

"Did you identify the girl you found with the Rays?" the vice president asked.

"We dusted the house for prints before the police arrived, but came up blank." Victor shook his head. We also took a couple of pictures of her in Charlie's window the night before, but it was too dark to make out her features properly." He spread meaty hands. "We have no idea who she is."

"Could she just be Charlie's girlfriend?" Mrs Magdalene mulled over what she had been told. "In the wrong place at the wrong time?"

"No. In my opinion, she's more dangerous than the boy."

"If she didn't join in the fight, what leads you to that conclusion?"

"As soon as she showed up, all our bugs went dark. Naturally, we removed them after the family fled." Victor reached into his pocket and took out a small blackened object. "They're fried. Not turned off or disabled. Fried." He tossed the device onto the vice president's desk. "These things are state of the art. I don't know of anything that could reduce them to charred metal."

"Frankie could. He's also capable of scrubbing the girl's identity from any database." Mrs Magdalene gave a thin smile, though it turned into a sinister leer on the shattered side of her face. "I assumed he was destroyed too, but it looks like I was wrong. He must have been downloaded onto a chip or external drive. Judging by what you've said, I'm now inclined to believe this unidentified girl has it." She picked up the bug and studied it. "I don't like being wrong."

"And I have no idea who Frankie is." Victor sounded disapproving. "I could have done my job better if I'd had all the facts."

Mrs Magdalene stared at him.

"Don't you *ever* criticise me."

She got up and clumped round the desk. Her legs were as burned and twisted as her visage, encased in an exoskeleton of shining rods and pistons. They made a hissing noise when she walked.

Victor watched her warily.

"I want those children hunted down," the vice president growled. "All of Manticorps' resources will be at your disposal, and I'm putting you in charge of a new team. A very *special* team."

"With all due respect, ma'am, my old squad are up to that task."

"Forget about them. They've been... retired."

Victor knew 'retired' meant dead, but he showed no emotion. In his line of work, sentiments got you killed.

"Whatever secrets those brats are carrying, they belong to Manticorps," the vice president seethed. "They're our *property*." She removed her glove, revealing a skeletal hand made of burnished steel. It looked like some horrible metal spider attached to her wrist. "Yet... you let them escape." She grabbed Victor by the throat and squeezed until his eyes bulged.

The man fought for breath but didn't struggle or look away. Instead, he slid his own hand inside his jacket.

"See, *that's* why you're still in charge, Vic." Mrs Magdalene looked down at the revolver pressed against her stomach. "You don't panic easily." She let go of his neck and grasped the gun. Spindly fingers tightened on the weapon and crumpled it like paper. "But, if you ever let me down again, I'll do the same thing to your head."

Part 2

The Scheme

To achieve great things, two things are needed:
a plan and not quite enough time.

– Leonard Bernstein

Leaning on the balcony rail, Charlie watched gathering clouds scudding across the sky, almost scraping the hilltops. Every now and then the sun broke through, intensifying the colour of patchwork fields. Yet the beauty of the landscape was lost on him.

He had a vague idea forming but no clue how to put it into practise and the notion of failure made him feel physically ill. "Don't get all dark and gloomy," he repeated over and over. "Remember your favourite holiday or something."

That just made things worse. Holidays had always been with his mum and dad, people he loved but now realised he barely knew and might never see again. Despite Daffodil's reassurances, he felt utterly alone.

What was Frankie playing at? Who could believe a teenager, no matter how smart, was capable of carrying out a prison break?

The boy's eyes widened.

Who *would* believe that? Certainly no one at Sunnyside.

His mind began to jump. He sat down and wrote:

Physically ill. Who would suspect a teenager? Stick together.

And suddenly he had the rest of his plan.

Charlie came back into the living room, carrying a sheaf of notes covered in scribbled handwriting.

"You been on that balcony for two hours." Daffodil was staring at the TV. "Writin your life story or somethin?"

"My life story wouldn't take *one* hour. And the only exciting bit would be the last couple of days." He dumped his notes on the table. "I've been thinking a lot about that. Not that I wouldn't go back to how things were."

"I had a go at a plan myself. But I got distracted by this television thingie." Daffodil switched off the set. "Didn't realise what a terrible state the world was in."

"Ah," Charlie said. "You've been watching the news."

"Nah. Somethin called *Britain's Got Talent*."

"You are genuinely strange." He grabbed the sheaf and handed it over. "Read this."

"You've perked up a bit."

"I've been scared to use my new-found powers, but that's definitely the wrong approach in this situation." He twiddled his thumbs sheepishly. "Maybe I've tried a bit *too* hard to be normal, in fact. Might have made me a bit… boring."

"You'll get no argument from me. You're about as square as a dice in a box factory."

"Thanks. Thing is, whether my ability is a talent or a curse, I'll have to use it for this job. Win or lose, you won't hear any more complaints."

"Especially if we lose. Then everyone will be dead."

"Yeah. Always look on the bright side. Now read."

Daffodil went through the pages slowly. Charlie shuffled around impatiently until she was finished.

"This is your big scheme, huh?" She put down the papers. "I got a few choice words to describe it."

"Ready and waiting."

"Insane."

"That's one word."

"OK. It's completely and utterly insane. Also, preposterous, far-fetched and ludicrous." She shrugged. "Frankie has been expandin my repertoire of put-downs."

"Oh." Charlie's face fell. "I... thought you'd like the idea."

"Have you met me?" Daffodil tweaked his nose. "I love it!"

"Stop that right now and let's talk to Frankie." The boy prised himself away and turned on the computer.

"Time to find out how good *he* is."

"Some of the items you want are difficult to get hold of." The screen flashed up a large exclamation mark. "And by difficult, I mean damned near impossible."

"Can't you order them on the web?" Charlie asked. "Have them secretly delivered?"

"I'm pretty sure Amazon doesn't sell bazookas."

"Ignore that one." Daffodil chuckled. "I slipped it in for a laugh."

"Fortunately, I anticipated you might need specialised equipment, so Gerry and I already made preparations. You can bask in my awesomeness later."

"It's great you're always thinkin two steps ahead," Daffodil said. "But you couldn't possibly have some of the things Chaz is askin for."

"A bit of faith please." Frankie's lights twinkled merrily. "Meet me in the basement."

"We have a basement?"

"It's why I picked this house. There's a trapdoor in the hall cupboard."

Minutes later, Charlie and Daffodil had descended a ladder and were standing in a vast concrete bunker running the length of the house. Wooden tables covered in vials and bottles were dotted around, along with implements and tools they didn't recognise. Another computer screen was fastened to the wall, blue ovals flickering across its surface.

"What is all this?" Charlie asked.

"It's the Manticorps Marginal Division research lab, or as near a recreation as Gerry and I could manage. In fact, it's better. Most of the projects those amateurs were researching hadn't even reached development stage. I got Gerry to make some modifications and now they actually work." Frankie sounded smug. "He might look like the world's oldest cockatoo nowadays, but your dad's pretty capable when it comes to technology. Check this out."

The glowing dots formed an arrow on the screen, pointing to the far end of the room. On the floor was a huge white object with a silver handle on the door.

"It's a fridge," the boy scoffed. "Big deal."

"It's a three-dimensional printer. Heard of them, Chaz? Or do you still use crayons and a whiteboard?"

"You use it to print actual objects instead of just words on paper." Charlie remembered seeing a programme about it. "I still can't get my head round that. But I do know they're pretty basic."

"Not the one I designed. Want a demonstration?"

"Sure," Daffodil said. "I'll have a double-fudge sundae with chocolate sprinkles. And a pony."

"Put it on your birthday list."

"I would if I knew when my goddamned birthday was."

"All in good time. Right now I'm hacking into the Department of Motor Vehicles database."

Frankie paused dramatically. "And sending that information to the printer."

The machine began to whir.

"It extracts elements from the air and combines them, layer upon layer, until it makes an exact replica of whatever you want. Cool, huh?"

The box pinged and the door opened. Two yellow rectangles lay inside.

"Fake number plates for the van in the garage, as you requested. I can also produce paint, so you can respray it and have transport that won't be recognised. The vehicle already has tinted windows, so nobody will see there are only kids inside."

"Nice of Manticorps to give us a van filled with the latest technology and surveillance equipment," Charlie said appreciatively. "That'll come in handy."

"I can also hack Sunnyside's databases to give you plans of the prison, the location of each inmate and details about the guards and other staff."

"Please do that. Can you give me a rough overview right now?"

"Natch." The screen gave a thumbs-up emoji. "The facility has two hundred warders and the White Spider is in an isolation block, reserved for the most dangerous criminals. The cells and corridors have doors with electronic locks that I can open and close, but once you leave the wing you'll have to cross a large central compound to reach the main gate."

"In full view of any guards outside?"

"Unfortunately, yes. Plus the gate has double-reinforced steel doors. They aren't electronic, so I can't move them. And the wall is fifteen feet high with barbed wire on top."

"Can you shut down the alarms?"

"Most of them, but there are hand-cranked sirens in the event of a power cut. They go off and squad cars full of armed response officers will be on the scene within ten minutes. Any inmate actually making it past them will be hunted by police helicopters and tracker dogs."

"Much as I hate to agree with Chaz," Daffodil breathed, "this *is* impossible."

"No." Charlie held up his hand. "It's pretty much as I expected. What about the last thing I asked for?"

"The chemical compound? Nothing like that has ever been invented. I'd have to work out a very intricate formula from scratch."

"Oh." The boy couldn't hide his disappointment. "How long will it take?"

"Might be up to an hour."

"I didn't like you at first, Frankie, but you're growing on me."

"Same here. Fancy starting a book club?"

"Don't push it."

Daffodil glanced at Charlie as though she was waiting for him to say something about her, but he was busy investigating the room. She gave a sigh and joined in. "Hey, I found a second printer." She opened the door of another white box. "Wow! You replicated bottles of Coke."

"That is a fridge."

"Oh." She blushed. "Can I have one?"

"Knock yourself out. Don't drink the stuff myself. Distinct lack of lips."

"Back to business," Charlie commanded. "Can you look like a human being, Frankie? On the screen, I mean."

"Why? What's wrong with the way I am?"

"I'd like to have an actual person to talk to."

"If you insist. You and the printer aren't the only ones who can copy things. That was another pun, by the way."

The dots on the screen converged until a face appeared. It resembled Charlie, but had Daffodil's hair and eyes.

"How about this?" Frankie smiled maniacally. There was a huge gap between his two front teeth.

"Hahahahahah!" Daffodil elbowed her horrified companion. "If we had kids, that's what they'd look like!"

"I'm not even going there." Charlie peered through his fingers. "Please just go back to being shapes. And give us the low-down on the White Spider."

"The White Spider is a mercenary who fought for Manticorps in Iraq and Afghanistan."

A map of the Middle East flashed up on the screen.

"Apparently, he murdered his entire squad out there, though it was never proved. He snuck back to into Britain but couldn't adjust to civilian life. Got into a fight in some bar and killed three ex-servicemen with his bare hands. A thoroughly nasty piece of work."

"With a friend like that, who needs enemies?" Charlie gasped. "What if he bumps off someone else while he's on the loose?"

"He'll be a fugitive in hiding. He's not likely to stroll into Sainsbury's and start shooting the place up 'cause they don't have his favourite brand of cornflakes."

"Then he'd be a cereal killer," Daffodil guffawed.

"But you're happy to set him on the people at Manticorps," Charlie tutted. "If he hates them as much as you say, won't there be carnage?"

"I'll appeal to his better nature."

"I can never tell if you're joking." The boy glared at Frankie's screen. "I'm not sure you can either."

"Says the guy with a sense-of-humour bypass. Leave the

damage limitation to me. I can't give you-"

"Any more details than that. Way ahead of you." Charlie took a mask and spray gun from a rack on the wall. "Right now, I have a van to paint."

"And then?" Daffodil handed him a Coke.

"We break into a warehouse on the outskirts of Edinburgh." He took a swig. "There's something in there that we need for my plan to work."

The van, now painted jet black, drove silently through the back streets of Edinburgh. In the passenger seat, Daffodil had her eyes closed, a look of intense concentration on her face.

Charlie knew she was absorbing information from Frankie. Books. Movies. Dates. Famous people. Political movements. He assumed she was trying to replace the knowledge that had been eradicated from her mind when the chip was implanted.

"Ask him to give you the recipe for cheese scones," he said. "I'm a fiend for cheese scones."

"I'm a partner in crime, Chaz. Not your bloody chef."

The vehicle pulled to a stop outside a complex of large corrugated buildings surrounded by a high wire fence. Charlie cut the engine and switched off the lights. In the darkness, the black vehicle was nearly invisible. He reached behind the driver's seat and hauled a tin of liquid onto his lap.

"You want Warehouse 7: Empire Cleaning Products." Daffodil had a hand on her neck. "Frankie says to look for a bunch of blue plastic tanks labelled 'Promundus'. Put a splash of his special formula into each. That oughta do it." She lowered her voice. "What if the place is guarded?"

"There's nothing important enough in there to need a nightwatchman. Stay in the van and don't touch anything."

Charlie got out of the vehicle and scaled the fence, container in one hand.

Daffodil watched as he crept over to the window of Warehouse 7. It was beyond his reach, so the boy balanced several discarded wooden crates underneath and clambered up. There was a soft tinkle of breaking glass and he vanished inside.

"'Stay in the van and don't touch anything.'" She mimicked her partner's voice. "When are you gonna stop treating me like some kinda lackey?" She unwrapped corned beef sandwiches she had brought for the wait and took a bite. "Seemsh like you and Frankie don't hardly need me any more." She chewed angrily. "Well, I'm jusht ash valuable a part of thish team ash you two."

She leaned on the steering wheel and the horn beeped loudly.

"No, no!" Daffodil dropped the sandwich in horror and it landed on the dirty floor. "Guess I really am useless. Can't do nothin right."

She looked out of the window to see if anyone had been alerted by the noise. "What the…?"

Three ominous shapes flitted along the side of the buildings, low to the ground, and stopped under the window that was Charlie's way in and out.

"Dobermans!" Daffodil winced. "We are officially knee-deep in doggie doo."

The hounds lay down behind the pile of wooden crates and waited for Charlie to emerge again.

"No wonder this place don't need a nightwatchman." Daffodil jumped out of the van. "Chaz ain't gonna see those mutts till it's too late."

She picked up her sandwiches, ran to the fence and quickly

climbed to the top. The Dobermans spotted her and dashed towards the new intruder.

Daffodil threw the bread slices as hard as she could. They landed several yards away and the dogs rushed over to devour them. The warehouse window creaked open and Charlie began to wriggle through the gap.

"Guard dogs!" she hissed. "Stay where you are, buddy, or your butt's gonna get munched!"

He shot her a look of panic. "What'll I do?"

"Nothin as stupid as this, I hope."

Daffodil leapt from the top of the fence and landed in the enclosure with a grunt. Then she was on her feet and running towards Charlie. The dogs abandoned the sandwiches and raced after her. She scrambled up the pile of crates with the animals snapping at her heels.

"You're the muscle, Chaz," she wheezed, as Charlie pulled her to safety. "Can you take 'em?"

"Not three monsters that size," he gulped. "Besides, I'm... eh... scared of dogs. It's more of a phobia really."

"Oh, that's *fantastic*. I've been sittin thinkin you're tougher than a hobnail boot in a pickle jar and you suddenly have a weak spot."

"The van's filled with surveillance equipment," Charlie said hopefully. "Can Frankie transmit a high-frequency signal that will hurt those dog's ears enough to drive them away?"

"He says animals don't hear radio waves." Daffodil shook her head. "A really loud bang will scare them, but it'll also attract attention."

"We can't just sit here!" Charlie looked anxiously at the canines. "Every minute we hang around increases our chances of being discovered."

Daffodil held her neck and listened. "Well, I guess I'm the

84

expendable one." She grabbed the empty tin Charlie was still carrying, took a deep breath and jumped.

"Mac!" Charlie hissed. "What are you doing?"

Daffodil landed on one hound and smacked another across its snout with the metal can. The surprised creatures bounded away but stopped after a few yards. Then they turned and advanced, bellies scraping the ground and lips pulled menacingly back over their teeth.

The girl knelt and began scooping stones into the can, never taking her eyes off the dogs. They began to make tentative runs at her, before retreating again.

"Chaz? When they attack, head for the fence."

Charlie hesitated. But, no matter how scared he was, he couldn't let Daffodil face the creatures alone.

"The hell I will." He jumped down and landed beside her, sending up a puff of dirt. "Ladies first."

"How very old-fashioned." The girl stood up. "But, according to Frankie, sometimes old-fashioned works." She began to shake the tin. The stones bounced around inside, making a hollow booming noise. The Dobermans began to back away, whining and pawing the dirt. "Sounds like thunder, don't it?" Daffodil moved forwards, still rattling the tin. "And pooches are terrified of thunder." She hurled the canister and the beasts took off again, genuinely frightened this time. "Go!"

She sprinted for the fence, her partner close behind. They reached the top as the creatures came racing back, leaping and snarling but unable to reach their quarry.

"Nice work, Mac." Charlie helped her over and down. "I owe you one."

"Can you go back for my sandwiches then? I'm starvin."

"Very funny. I'll make you a pizza when we get home."

"That was a neat trick back there." Charlie hunched over the wheel on the drive back to Bellbowrie. "Quick thinking too."

"I ain't just a pretty face, Chaz." Daffodil batted her eyelids.

"Don't believe I mentioned your looks."

"You're a master at shuttin people out, know that?"

"Why didn't Frankie warn us about the dogs?" The boy shifted gears as smoothly as the subject.

"He doesn't want too many details, remember? So I didn't tell him exactly what we were gonna do." She scratched her cheek. "It just proves we can't always depend on him to fix things. We really are on our own."

They drove in silence for a while.

"You risked your life for me," Charlie said eventually. "After I've been so rotten to you."

"That mean you're gonna be nice from now on?"

"Nah. You're still a royal pain."

"Don't matter." Daffodil grinned. "You risked your life for me too."

"Can't allow you to die just yet. You're part of my cunning plan."

"In other words, we're a team."

"All right," Charlie sighed. "We're a team."

"Then we should have a name." Daffodil's smile widened. "Like the Dynamic Duo." She tapped her fingers together. "I know. The Army of Two!"

"That's an X-Box game."

"Still dunno what an X-Box is, but I'll take your word for it." The girl thought for a while.

"How about the Armageddon Twins?"

"That *is* catchy," Charlie conceded. "As long as people don't think we're actually related."

"The Armageddon Twins." Daffodil took up a fighting stance. "Saving the world, one mistake at a time." She punched out at an invisible enemy. "Pow! Pow!"

"Don't make me regret agreeing to this."

"We should have capes. And masks." She giggled. "I got a pair of tights you can wear."

"Please stop."

"We can get business cards printed."

"If I can get a word in, I was going apologise." Charlie drove up the driveway of their house and pulled into the garage. "I never really thought about how it must feel. Not remembering who you are."

"Pretty crappy. But I reckon little bits are startin to come back."

"Really? Like what?"

"I think I used to live in a big house," Daffodil said wistfully. "A mansion, in fact. I reckon I might have been pretty well off."

"Anything else?"

"It had a library. All polished wood and leather couches. I used to spend hours readin anythin I could get my hands on. Old detective novels were my favourite." She thought hard. "Nope. It's all pretty hazy and I can't recall anythin else." She shrugged.

"Frankie promised to tell me everythin when this is over, so I guess I'll just have to wait."

"He seems to have warmed to us, but I still don't trust him." Charlie switched off the ignition. "I'm going to do a little digging of my own, when I get the chance."

"You ain't got much to go on. I'm a bit of an enigma."

"True. But I can't see a good reason why he'd keep your past secret. Not now that you're committed to helping." He looked at her quizzically. "Unless there's something terrible lurking there."

"Very tactful." Daffodil sighed. "You sure know how to sweet-talk a girl."

"I've got oodles of charm, haven't I?"

"Actually, you *can* be quite charismatic when it suits you."

"Frankie teaching you big words again?"

"Chaz." Daffodil laid a hand on his arm. "I gotta ask. How come I never seen you laugh? Or even smile?"

The boy glanced at her, and for a second it looked like he might answer. Then the moment passed.

"C'mon, Mac." He jumped out and opened the passenger door. "Let's make dinner."

"So you made it back in one piece?" Frankie swirled around the computer screen as a series of triangles.

"We did good, buddy." Daffodil mumbled through a mouthful of pizza. "What's next?"

"Ask Charlie. He's the boss in this caper."

Charlie was already leafing through the sheets of information on Sunnyside's staff and inmates that Frankie had printed out. He picked out a picture of a young red-headed woman.

"Samantha McLaren. A nurse in the prison infirmary." He helped himself to another slice. "She's perfect."

"Care to elaborate?"

"According to your data, she's in trouble. We can use her and help her at the same time."

"You're *enjoyin* this!" Daffodil looked hard at Charlie. "You been sittin in the sun? You're thawing. Or is the real you go-gettin as well as grouchy?"

"Just trying to come up with the best scheme I can," Charlie retorted. "If I do something decent for this woman at the same time, isn't that a good thing?"

"It's a great thing." Daffodil winked at him. "Bit heroic actually."

Charlie blushed. To cover his embarrassment, he rifled through more pages and selected the mug shot of a handsome man holding up a card with his prison number stencilled on it. "And we'll want this guy. Scotty Primo. Another inmate at Sunnyside."

"He's a grifter," Daffodil said. "A con man."

"How did you know that?" Frankie inquired.

"No scars on his face or knuckles, so he's not into violence. His hands ain't got calluses, so his crimes don't involve anything physical. Dude's hair is neatly combed and he's posing worse than a male model, even in a mug shot. He's careful about his appearance." She picked up Primo's folder. "This is a guy who uses looks and charisma to get what he wants."

"That was very perceptive. I'm impressed."

"I've read a ton of detective novels. Plus, I'm understudyin for Chaz in case he gets eaten by dogs."

"Very funny."

"Primo's doing ten years." Daffodil whistled. "That's a pretty big sentence for a scam artist."

"It's because he conned some very rich people out of a lot of money and won't say where it's stashed." Charlie pinned the pictures to the basement wall. "We need the help of both these people if my plan is going to work."

"What if they won't play ball?"

"They will if we push the right buttons."

"I can't allow you to harm anyone," Frankie warned. "Told you already."

"I've no intention of hurting them. Quite the opposite." Charlie wiped a string of cheese from his chin. "Frankie, I'll need cash. A lot of cash."

"I can hack any bank account undetected. Already donated a few Russian mobsters' life savings to Amnesty International, as a matter of fact."

"I've got some new villains lined up to steal money from." Charlie began to tidy away the plates. "Then I'll deal with Samantha McLaren. Daffodil?"

"Yup?"

"You're going to have a little chat with Mr Primo. Frankie will tell you what to say."

"I ain't a glove puppet, Chaz." She pinged an olive at him. "I'm quite capable of doin my own talkin. In fact, I never shut up."

"Yeah. I had noticed." Charlie shuffled the papers into a neat pile. "Next stop? Sunnyside."

16

Daffodil presented her fake ID to the reception desk of Sunnyside Prison.

"This is very unusual." The receptionist looked disconcerted. "Unaccompanied children aren't normally permitted to make visits."

"My mother and I are only in the country a short while and she isn't feelin too great." Daffodil handed over a permission slip. "So the Home Office made an exception."

"Oh. Well, these look to be in order." The woman studied the perfectly forged papers that Frankie had printed. "You'll have to be searched for contraband, even if you are a minor."

"That's all right." Daffodil allowed herself to be frisked then walked through the scanner. She half expected the chip in her neck to set off the alarm, but Frankie was encased in plastic and invisible to the detection devices. Her picture was taken and she was given a visitor pass to clip on.

"All done." The warder on duty ushered her through.

"This security system sucks," Frankie muttered in her head. "They deserve to lose a prisoner or two. Maybe it'll persuade them to try a bit harder in the future."

Scotty Primo was led to a small plastic table in the visitor room.

"You don't get company very often." The guard sat him down. "And you never mentioned having a daughter before."

"First time she's ever set foot in the place, boss." Scotty said dolefully. "I haven't seen her in years."

"Tough break." The man shrugged and walked off. Everyone in here had a hard-luck story and he'd heard them all before.

The door opened with a buzz and a girl dressed in black edged in. Spotting Scotty, she rushed across the room and squeezed him tightly. "Hello, Dad!"

"Hi, darling. Take a seat." Scotty glanced round to make sure the guard wasn't listening, but he was already engrossed in conversation with one of his workmates. "I'm an inquisitive type," Scotty was well spoken and his piercing green eyes rarely blinked. "Which is why I agreed to this request for a visit. Problem is, you're not my daughter. Her mum won't let her see me until she turns sixteen and can decide for herself."

"Can't imagine why." The girl snapped her fingers. "Oh. Maybe 'cause you're a convicted criminal and probably not the best role model a young girl could have."

"OK. You've done your homework." Scotty nodded. "And you must have some pretty convincing documents or you wouldn't have made it through that door." He gave a smile and his eyes twinkled. It made him look both likeable and trustworthy. "I certainly appreciate the company, but I still want to know why you're pretending to be my kid."

"Dial down the charisma, bub. I ain't the swoonin type." The girl kept her voice low. "My name's Daffodil McNugget and—"

"That's a pretty stupid alias, if you don't mind me saying…" Scotty studied her face, then looked mortified. "Oh. You're telling the truth. Sorry."

"And my accomplices and I are gonna break you out," Daffodil continued, undeterred. "In return for a favour, of course."

"I've only got five years of my sentence left to serve," the man replied calmly. "I don't want to be broken out, even if it were possible."

"It's possible."

"No thanks." Primo turned to beckon the guard.

"I understand your reluctance. You *had* £5,000,000 you conned outta fat cats stashed in a bank account in the Cayman Islands. Only it's gone."

The smile vanished. "Say that again."

"Sort code 45 85 96. Account number 188722563148." Daffodil reeled off the numbers. "We emptied it."

Scotty's mouth opened, but no sound came out.

"That enough of an incentive for ya, buddy?"

"The money I hid was to set my daughter up in life," Primo replied acidly. "My *real* daughter."

"Then she's gonna be a damned sight poorer."

Scotty Primo was a practical man. This girl had his bank details and how she got them wasn't important right now. She was obviously a force to be reckoned with.

"You have my attention."

Daffodil slipped a hand inside her shirt, clicked open a hidden catch on her pendant, and removed three tiny pills. "These oughta be small enough to hide on your person." She took Scotty's hand and slid the capsules into his palm. "You swallow one and convince a convict called the White Spider to take the other. They'll give you a temperature and bring you out in a rash, but there won't be no long-term effects. However, they'll land you both in the prison infirmary and we'll be able to break you out from there."

"Then the answer's *definitely* no."

"No?" Daffodil was taken aback.

"I conned rich people. Nasty rich people." The man glared at her. "But I've never killed anyone. I'm certainly not helping put a sadistic animal like the White Spider back on the streets."

"I take it you don't like the guy."

"This place contains some of the most hardened criminals in the country," Scotty replied. "Men who have slaughtered women and children without blinking an eye. Guys who aren't afraid of anything." He shuddered. "Except the White Spider. He's sinister beyond words. He scares the *guards*, for God's sakes."

"He'll only be free for a short time. Then we'll turn him over to the police." Daffodil gave a sly wink. "Though you don't have to share *that* particular bit of info with him."

"You expect me to believe this nonsense?" Scotty laughed out loud and the prison officer looked round. "Just sharing a father–daughter joke, boss!"

"Nice to see you're getting along." The warder checked his watch. "You've got ten minutes left."

"Fine." Daffodil said nonchalantly. "There are a dozen inmates in here we can use instead."

"Then do so. This visit is over."

"All right. We'll put the money back into your account."

"You'll do what?" It was Scotty's turn to look flabbergasted.

"If you'd intended to keep your ill-gotten gains, we'd take the lot. But your daughter ain't a criminal, so it's not fair to deprive her of a decent life." She got up to leave. "Good to know you got *some* morals."

"Sit down." Scotty stared into her eyes. "I'm the best con man in the business and I always know when someone's playing me." He sat back and rubbed his head. "You're telling the *truth*."

"Here's somethin else to think about." The girl held his stare. "Your daughter don't need money. She needs a dad in her life."

"Yeah? What good is a father who's always looking over his shoulder in case the law closes in?"

"We'll provide you with a new identity and tell you where your daughter is, if you wanna risk seein her." Daffodil shrugged. "I sure hope you try."

"You don't know where *your* parents are, kid," Scotty said sympathetically. "Do you?"

"You're certainly good at reading people." The girl smiled sadly. "I don't even know *who* they are, but I'd give anything to find out."

"A great liar can always spot when someone is being insincere." The man ran a hand down his face. "And you're not."

"We're the good guys, Mr Primo. Honest."

"Who is the third pill for?"

"The prison doctor. Slip it into his drink when you get to the infirmary." She reddened slightly. "I hate to have an innocent man suffer but, like I say, it won't have no-long term effects. He'll be right as rain in a couple of days."

"I need to think about it."

"It's a one-time offer." She snapped her locket shut. "Turn me down and you'll have five long years to ponder your missed opportunity."

"You can really pull this off?"

"It should have been impossible for me to get this far. But here I am."

"I want to see my daughter more than you could imagine. So count me in." Scotty pocketed the pills. "But if this prison break goes wrong, I'll find a way to convince the authorities I was a victim and not an accomplice."

"I'm sure you will. You're slippier than a weasel coated in axle grease."

"Also, are you positive the White Spider *wants* out of jail?"

"Why wouldn't he? He's got a life sentence."

"Because he's completely off his rocker, by all accounts. He actually seems to like it here."

The girl took on a faraway look, as if she were listening to some voice Scotty couldn't hear.

"Time's up, people," the guard shouted.

"If he won't co-operate, tell him this." She leaned forward, kissed the man on the cheek and whispered a sentence in his ear.

"I don't even know what that means," Scotty said dubiously.

"It'll work. My source is never wrong."

She got up and left with the warder.

The grifter watched her go, fingering the pills in his pocket and wondering just what he had agreed to.

Daffodil climbed into the van, parked outside the prison gates.

"Primo's on board," she announced. "We can't take his money though. It's for his daughter."

"Are you sure he didn't con you about that?" Charlie was sitting behind the wheel. "It's what he does."

"Not at all," Daffodil replied. "But I gave my word and I ain't about to break it."

"That's all right. We have another bank account to empty. And this one belongs to a proper scumbag."

Charlie started the engine and drove off.

"My turn now. Tomorrow we're going to rescue Nurse Samantha McLaren from an extremely bad situation."

"You might want to consider something." Frankie spoke from one of the monitors in the back of the vehicle. "Nobody knows who Daffodil is, but I made the security cameras blurry, just in case. Her prints and ID will also vanish from Sunnyside's systems when this is over. You're a different kettle of fish, Charlie."

"In what way?"

"The shootout at your house has been on the news, along with your picture. I can wipe the CCTV near Miss McLaren's house, but a passer-by might still recognise you. You better wear a disguise."

"As long as it's nothing like my dad's effort," Charlie said. "Besides, I'm too young to grow a moustache."

"Ooh! Ooh! I know!" Daffodil held up her hand. "I got the perfect camouflage."

"This is bound to be good. What have you got in mind?"

She told them both her idea.

"I am *not* doing that," Charlie fumed. "No way. Not a chance."

"You're turning out to be quite an asset, Mac." Frankie laughed. "I'd pay serious money to see this."

"Not doing it," the boy repeated.

"Don't worry." Daffodil could hardly contain her glee. "You're gonna look adorable."

"I'll replicate the things we need. Sorry, Chaz."

"Daffodil?" Charlie glowered. "I really hate you right now."

17

Samantha McLaren sat on the couch, an arm round her young son. The doorbell rang and they both flinched.

"Hide in your room, honey." She patted the boy's head. "It'll be all right. I promise."

The child held on tight, refusing to let go.

"Please, Gus. I'll be fine."

Her son plodded tearfully through to his bedroom. Samantha went to the door and slowly opened it.

A diminutive, white-faced clown stood on the step, sporting a red rubber nose and painted-on grin. His head was topped by a huge orange wig and he wore a spotted suit with a frilly collar and giant flappy shoes. In one gloved hand he held a large tartan bag; in the other he clutched the strings of a bunch of balloons, which floated above his head like a multicoloured cloud.

"Miss McLaren?" he said glumly. "You've won two free tickets to the circus. Can I come in?"

"What?" Samantha couldn't believe her eyes. "Who *are* you?"

"The name's Charlie, but you can call me Chuckles."

"You have to go away, son. I don't want free tickets." Samantha looked nervously up and down the street. "I'm... I'm expecting visitors."

"Yes. You're waiting for Ryan Cardownie. He's a loan shark and you owe him several thousand pounds. Only you don't have the cash to pay him back."

"Oh." Samantha instantly turned hostile. "You work for him, you little monster."

"If I did, I wouldn't have turned up looking like I escaped from nutty town."

Charlie stuck his giant foot in the door before Samantha could shut it. "I'm actually here to pay off your debt." He opened the bag, stuffed to the brim with £100 notes. "Now may I come in?"

"Why would you help me?" Sammy sat on a chair opposite the stranger. "And how come you're dressed like that?"

"No time for discussion. Mr Cardownie is always prompt." Charlie looked at a big yellow watch decorated with ladybirds. "He'll be here any second."

"And then?"

"I'll make him go away." He curled up in his chair, trying to get his feet to behave. The balloons bobbed and swayed above him, bumping into the walls and ceiling. "You get into the bedroom with your son and let me handle things."

"Handle things?" Samantha couldn't believe her ears. "How old are you? Twelve? Thirteen?"

"I'm fourteen. And I'm not alone."

"Ryan Cardownie is a vicious thug and he'll have his gang with him." Samantha was close to tears. "There's much more in that bag than the amount I owe. He'll take it all."

"He'll certainly try." The boy waved her away. "You go and look after Gus. I imagine he's freaking out."

"I'm not leaving you with that guy. You're only a child!"

"Let's just say I have a rather unique set of skills."

"What? Making balloon animals?" She glared at him. "Wait.

99

Is this some kind of police sting, with you as the decoy?"

"That's absolutely right," Charlie retorted quickly, realising this was the perfect excuse for his presence.

"I don't see any unmarked vehicles parked out there." Samantha peeked round the curtains. "Just the usual cars."

"If you could spot a sting, so could Ryan," the boy pointed out. "We have a surveillance van in the next street and I'm wearing a wire."

The doorbell rang.

"It's him!" Samantha looked round in terror. "Oh God."

"Off you go," Charlie urged. "Don't come out until I tell you, no matter what kind of commotion you hear."

"Thank you, whoever you are." Samantha vanished into the bedroom.

The bell rang again, but Charlie ignored it. A few seconds later there was a crash as the front door was kicked open. Two men strode into the living room, led by Ryan Cardownie. Cardownie was well built, with slicked-down hair, a spotty face and an arrogant stance.

"Evening, gentlemen." Charlie raised a white-gloved hand in greeting. "I take it you've come about an unpaid debt?"

"Who the hell are you, Coco?" Ryan narrowed his eyes. "Why are you dressed like some freak?"

"I like to spread joy and happiness," the boy said dourly. "Got a problem with that?"

"I'll be happy when I get my cash. Where is it?"

"Miss McLaren owes you four grand." He pointed to the open bag on the table. "Take that amount and bugger off."

Ryan pulled the valise towards him and smirked nastily. "Unfortunately, my interest rate has suddenly just gone up, so I'll be having all of this." He rifled though the contents and gave a sharp intake of breath. "There are hundreds of thousands in here!"

"Six hundred thousand and forty pounds, to be accurate." Charlie corrected. "I'm sure you recognise the figure. It's the exact amount that *used* to be in your private account."

"This is *my* money?" Ryan went purple. "How…?"

"No matter what bank you use, we'll hack it." The boy shrugged. "Which means you're going to find it hard to pay your accomplices."

Cardownie's henchmen glanced at each other.

"Not now I've got it back, moron." Ryan motioned to his companions. "Let's do some serious damage to this midget."

"You don't want to take that route." Charlie held up a large pin. "It'll make me a very angry clown. And I'm not in the best of moods on *any* day."

"You're going to fight us with a needle?" Ryan closed in on him, his heavies close behind. "Now *that's* funny."

Charlie took a deep breath and held it, then reached up and popped a large red balloon. A puff of incandescent dust enveloped the loan shark and he reeled away, gagging and clawing at his throat.

The boy was on his gigantic feet in a second. A jet of acidic liquid squirted from a plastic daisy on his lapel and hit the first yob in the face. The man clutched at his eyes as Charlie jabbed the pin into his leg and twisted. He sank to his knees and shuffled away, groaning in pain.

The second assailant swung at his diminutive adversary, but he ducked, pulled a rubber chicken from his voluminous pocket and smacked the man across the head. The thug flew backwards, smashing through the glass coffee table, unconscious before he landed.

"Got an iron bar inside," Charlie explained, knocking out the first yob as he tried to crawl to safety. "Your turn now, Cardownie."

"Get away from me!" The loan shark ran round the broken table, coughing and gasping, with Charlie waddling in pursuit, his enormous feet flapping on the carpet. He leapt into the air and landed on the man's back, arms round his neck. He tightened his grip and held on until Ryan collapsed and passed out.

"This is so undignified. I should have run away and joined the library instead."

He took a pair of plastic garden ties from his other pocket and fastened Ryan's hands behind his back. Then he grabbed a vase from the windowsill and poured water over him.

"I will kill you for this!" The loan shark sat up, spluttering and shaking his head. "You'll *never* be safe."

"You don't even know what I look like under this make-up." Charlie pushed the brute down and sat on him. "Thing is, that smart TV in the corner has a video cam, which my accomplice is controlling. Tomorrow I'm going to post our little fight on YouTube, along with your name and address."

"You wouldn't dare!" Ryan tried to buck him off.

"Nobody will spot the toxic gas I used on you," the boy said. "It's almost invisible. What they'll see is Ryan Cardownie and his mates roughed up by a kid in a clown suit. You'll never be able to intimidate anyone again." He leaned closer. "If that's not enough, we also recorded you telling your henchmen to beat up a child. That'll land you quite a stretch in prison. And you can't afford a good lawyer any more."

Ryan stopped struggling. "What do you want?"

"I want you to leave this family alone, get out of town, and never come back." Charlie held his pin to the man's throat.

"Because, if you do, my associates will be waiting. And *they* don't clown around."

"Look, we can work out a deal—"

"In your dreams." He whacked Ryan over the head with the chicken. "Goodnight."

"You seem to have everythin sewn up." Daffodil strolled in and fastened a strip of tape over Ryan's mouth. "I'll hog-tie the other two, though it don't look like they'll wake any time soon. When they do, it'll take them a few hours to get free."

"Thanks, Mac."

Charlie picked up the bag and clumped into the bedroom. Samantha McLaren was on the bed with her son. The child was sobbing into her shoulder.

"You won't be bothered by those louts again." He dropped the tartan holdall. "In this bag is £600,000 and some loose change. Take it and go start a new life."

"You're not with the police, are you?" Samantha's eyes were red-rimmed.

"Does it matter?"

"And you don't want anything in return? For all that money?"

"Send me a postcard. I hear the south of France is a nice place to live."

"I only got in debt because I wanted a few decent things for my boy." Samantha got up and squeezed her son tightly. "I don't make much on a hospital salary."

"No need to explain."

"C'mon, Gus." The woman pulled the boy to his feet. "Let's get out of this terrible place."

"Thank you, Mr Clown," the child said. "For helping my mum."

"Seems I'm in the saving business, whether I want to be or not." Charlie patted his head. "Pack anything important to you, but make it quick. You have enough cash to buy whatever else you need."

"This is my mobile number." Samantha scribbled on a piece of paper and handed it to him. "If you ever need anything, just call. Unless I'm in the Bahamas."

"Much obliged." The boy tucked it into a spotty pocket.

He waited until the pair left. Then he went back to the living room, sat on Ryan again and dialled the Sunnyside prison switchboard.

"This is Samantha McLaren," he said, imitating the woman's voice perfectly. "I need Warden Bishop to call me at home immediately. It's an emergency."

He hung up and waited. After a few minutes, the phone rang and he picked it up.

"This is Warden Bishop. What's wrong, Samantha?"

"You use a product called Promundus in the soap dispensers at Sunnyside." Charlie continued to impersonate the nurse. "Don't you?"

"I believe so. Why?"

"Because I work in the infirmary, I use it more than anyone else." He coughed for effect. "For the first time, it's given me a really nasty rash. I think it might be a bad batch."

"Are you all right?"

"I'll live. But, to be on the safe side, can you dump what you have and order a new supply immediately? I'd do it myself, only it looks like I'm going to be bed-bound for a few days."

"That'll be expensive."

"It'll be a lot more expensive if all your guards start calling in sick."

"True." The warden sounded suitably concerned. "I'll get it done right away. Thank you for alerting me and get well soon."

"I appreciate your concern." Charlie set the receiver down. Daffodil was watching him from the doorway.

"Well?"

"Next phase is complete. Now we have to repaint the van." He began to struggle out of his costume. "In two days we break the White Spider out of jail."

The White Spider sat on his own in Sunnyside's exercise yard, perched on a bench with his back to the wire fence, reading a book. He was a tall, sinewy man with a shaved head, bug eyes and thin, cruel lips. Nobody came near or tried to engage him in conversation, for his temper was as legendary as his fighting ability. Not long ago a convict called Carl Wicks had tried to make a reputation for himself by ambushing the Spider, backed by three of Sunnyside's most vicious hard men. All were carrying home-made weapons.

He was now known as One-eyed Wicks, and his accomplices hadn't fared much better.

Scotty shuddered at the thought of getting close to this lunatic, but he had no choice. He straightened his shoulders and walked over, trying to act cool and collected.

The White Spider glanced up as Primo approached and sat down next to him. "I have no wish to be disturbed, my good man." His tone was crisp. "I intend to finish this volume by lunchtime."

"And I've got no desire to disturb you." Scotty flashed his most disarming smile. "It's just that I have a proposition."

"I shall not warn you again." The White Spider went back to his paperback. "Your very presence is irritating me."

Scotty was an expert at quickly sizing people up. This maniac required a short, direct approach.

"I recently received a visit from a fourteen-year-old girl," he said. "She offered to break you and me out of prison in the next few days. Nobody else. Just us."

"That does sound intriguing," the Spider conceded. "Though I'm surprised a seasoned con artist like yourself would believe such a far-fetched notion. Especially one put to you by a mere child."

"She was extremely persuasive and I'm certain she has some serious backing." Scotty wasn't surprised that the Spider knew who he was. The creep seemed to be aware of everything that went on in Sunnyside. "As you pointed out," he continued, "I'm a con man and not the type to fall for a scam."

The Spider shut the book, his interest piqued.

"Did this girl tell you her plan?"

"She didn't have the opportunity to say much, but she gave me these." Scotty opened his palm to reveal two pills. "If we take them, it'll make us look sick enough to be moved to the infirmary. Her accomplices can break us out from there."

He felt a sharp pain in his leg and looked down.

The Spider was pressing a six-inch nail against his knee.

"The last time someone persuaded me to take a strange pill, it landed me in *this* establishment," he rasped. "So you have until the count of three to provide me with actual information. Or you will walk with a limp for the rest of your exceedingly short life."

"That's all I know!" Scotty spluttered, sweat beading his forehead. "I'm just passing on what she said."

"One."

"OK! She also gave me a message that I was to repeat to you."

"Two."

"She said she needed your help taking on Manticorps. Only I don't know who Manticorps are. Honestly!"

"Did she now?" The nail vanished up the Spider's sleeve. "Those were the exact words she uttered?"

"Wasn't hard to memorise."

"Hmm." He opened the book again, suddenly a model of politeness. "Have you read this? It's called *Groundworks for the Metaphysics of Morals* by the German philosopher Immanuel Kant. Quite fascinating."

"No," Scotty replied apprehensively. "I mostly like historical romances."

"If I may quote from Kant..." The Spider closed his eyes and recited. "'One who makes himself a worm cannot complain afterwards if people step on him.'"

"Eh... OK."

The Spider took his pill, slid it between two pages and snapped the volume shut.

"I shall make my intentions plainer," he said pleasantly. "I graciously accept your offer to remove myself from Sunnyside. If you are attempting to make a fool of me, however, I will grind you under the heel of my boot until you are dust." He stood up. "I look forward to seeing you in the infirmary. Try not to be tardy. I am not known for my patience."

He left without a backwards glance, leaving Scotty sitting rigid with fear.

Victor followed Mrs Magdalene down a long corridor.

"Capturing Charlie Ray and that girl, whoever she is, has become Manticorps' highest priority," the vice president said. "They're our only hope for retrieving Frankie and the Atlas Serum and putting our projects back on track."

She opened the door to the briefing room. Two men and one woman sat round the table, looking expectantly at them.

"This is your new team," the vice president said. "I'll let them introduce themselves."

"Markus Gantz." A young man with a crew cut, glasses and a T-shirt with 'FREE HUGS' written on it stood up and extended his hand. "I am pleased to meet you."

"I'm not." Victor didn't move. "Just tell me what you do."

"I am a hacker. Nobody knows computer systems better than I."

"Frankie does," Victor countered. "I've read the files and, apparently, part of him *is* a computer. You only sound like one."

"And you sound like a very negative guy." Markus sat back down. "I do not think we will be friends."

"No free hug, then? My heart bleeds."

Victor nodded to the woman. She was stunningly beautiful, with an innocent face and wide cobalt-blue eyes.

"What about you, blondie? In charge of make-up?"

"Candy-Anne." She studied her pointed nails. "I... retire people."

"That so?" Victor tensed.

"Make another sexist comment and I'll demonstrate." She fluttered her eyelids. "I'm a lot more than an extremely pretty face."

Victor turned to the last member. He was almost as large as the leader, with long, jet-black hair tucked under a baseball cap. Round his hand was a length of chain.

"You are?"

"Hill Rylander," the man replied laconically. "I'm a tracker. Old-school. If Markus can identify a rough location where the kids are holed up, I'll do the rest."

"How?" Victor was unimpressed. "You going to sniff the ground? Follow a trail of broken leaves?"

"Not me, chief." Hill pulled on the chain and a large white shape emerged from under the table. "Meet Willie."

Victor repressed a shudder. The huge dog was white and hairless, with malevolent pink eyes and jaws that looked like they could take a chunk out of solid metal. It glared at him and gave a throaty growl.

"Jeez." He quickly regained his composure. "Bit of an ugly brute."

"You don't want to antagonise Willie." Hill covered the dog's pointy ears. "He's very sensitive."

"I was talking about you."

"Willie was a normal pooch at one time," Mrs Magdalene said. "Until we tested our version of the Atlas Serum on him."

"I can see why you're so keen to have the perfected formula back." Victor regarded the mutant hound with distaste. "The old batch has a few nasty side effects."

"It does," the vice president accepted. "But now Willie has a nose that can pick out an individual in a crowded football stadium."

"Find out where the fugitives might be and let him get the scent." Hill patted the slavering beast. "He'll track them to the ends of the earth."

"As long as you three follow him, I'll be satisfied," Victor said sourly.

"I thought we were chasing kids, Mrs M," Candy-Anne said softly. "Not being led by one."

"Victor was quite attached to his old squad," the vice president explained, "but his bark is worse than his bite."

"Quite the opposite of Willie, then," Hill remarked. "I know which one I prefer."

"I'll leave you to it." Mrs Magdalene turned to go. "Stop moping and play nice, Victor."

"That dog will tear the kids apart," the giant said. "I assumed you wanted them in one piece."

"Charlie's blood is all we require to extract the perfected serum," Mrs Magdalene shot back. "And I imagine Frankie is on a USB or hard drive in the girl's possession. I simply want that returned."

"Yes. It is Frankie we really want to get hold of." Markus took off his glasses and wiped them. "If this artificial intelligence is as good as you claim, it will be able to replicate all Manticorps' lost research. I will extract that information from him. Never fear."

"So we don't need the kids alive." The vice president shrugged. "If they resist, you can kill them."

"I was hoping you'd say that," Candy-Anne said impishly. "Or else I'd have nothing fun to do."

Part 3

The Breakout

I keep my valuable things locked up.
Everyone does. Therefore, prisoners
must be valuable.

– Jarod Kintz

At five o'clock, Daffodil was led into the waiting room of Sunnyside prison, carrying a bunch of flowers. Once again she handed the receptionist her fake ID and permission slips. "I'm here to visit my dad," she said. "Scotty Primo."

"You didn't get our phone message?" The woman behind the desk looked distressed. "He's in the prison infirmary."

"The infirmary?" Daffodil feigned surprise. "Is he all right?"

"He has a temperature and a rash," the receptionist said. "So, I'm afraid you can't see him. Visits can only be conducted in the communal area."

"But I'm going back to Africa with my mother tomorrow. She works in a hospital there. It's my last chance."

"Those are the rules, I'm afraid."

"I brought him roses." Daffodil's lip quivered.

"I'm really sorry."

The girl burst into tears. "I came all the way from Aberdeen by myself on the train," she sobbed. "If I go back now, nobody will come to meet me for hours."

"There's nothing I can do, petal," the woman replied wretchedly. "It's protocol."

"But I wanted to say goodbye," Daffodil wailed, laying it on as thick as she dared. "I never told him I loved him and now he's sick."

Two guards turned from their conversation and walked over.

"It's all right, Muriel." The older guard laid a hand on the receptionist's arm. "Once the girl's been scanned and searched, I'll get Jake here to escort her."

His companion nodded assent.

"Primo's a model prisoner and this kid can't be more than fourteen. It's not like she has a crowbar in those flowers." He patted Daffodil's head. "Though you *will* have to leave the bouquet behind. Just in case."

"The White Spider is in the infirmary too, sir," Muriel hissed. "He's *not* a model prisoner."

"That creep is in another room under heavy restraint," the older guard replied calmly. "I can authorise it if you call the warden and let him know. He's got a daughter about the same age. He'll understand."

"On you go then, love." Muriel stamped Daffodil's papers. "I suppose I'm being a worry wart."

"C'mon, kid." The junior guard beckoned to her. "Let's get you to your father."

They walked down the corridors together, the girl making a mental note of where everything was. While Jake's back was turned, she held her breath until her face was red.

"You alright?" He glanced round. "You're all sweating and flushed."

"I don't feel too good," Daffodil slowly exhaled, throwing in a dramatic shiver for effect. "I hope I didn't make my dad ill. I visited him a couple of days ago."

"I'm sure it'll be fine." All the same, the guard quickened his step, putting a few feet between himself and his escort. "Just don't sneeze on me. I got holidays coming up."

The phone rang in Warden Bishop's office.

"Yes?"

"It's the Health Protection Agency in Collindale." The warden's secretary sounded alarmed. "They need to speak to you urgently."

"Put them through."

In the van, parked three miles away, Charlie was ready and waiting, mobile in hand.

"This is Douglas Livingstone from the HPA," he said in a deep baritone voice that he'd copied from the star of a medical drama on TV. "I understand you have a nurse working for you called Samantha McLaren."

"We do," the warden replied. "She's off sick."

"I'll make this brief. We've just been at her house and suspect she has a virulent form of the James River Fever. It's highly contagious and we can't work out how she got it. It's usually confined to remote regions of central Africa."

The warden thought for a few moments. Then he paled. "There was a girl called Audrey Primo here a couple of days ago, visiting her father. Her papers said she'd recently been in Africa, where her mum works in a... hospital."

"Oh dear," Charlie said. "Just the place to pick up this disease."

"Now her dad's in the prison infirmary." The warden hesitated. "And so is Audrey. She arrived a little while ago to see him."

"Good. If she's the carrier we need to keep her confined. Does Primo have a temperature and a rash?"

"Yes. The doctor on call has the same symptoms, and so does another inmate." The warden licked his lips nervously. "They're *all* in there."

"Then don't let anyone else in or out of the infirmary until we check this situation. The James River Fever is a real nasty one."

"I'll need to confirm your identity, you understand."

"Of course. Call the HPA right now and ask for extension 25."

The phone went dead.

Warden Bishop hit the intercom button with trembling fingers. "Look up the number for the Health Protection Agency and put me through," he commanded. "Now!"

Charlie sat in the surveillance vehicle, biting his nails while Frankie watched him from the screen, which showed an emoji of a Mexican bandit in a sombrero.

"Why are you projecting that?" the boy goggled.

"I'm undercover, aren't I?"

"Nobody but me can see you."

"Yeah. But I'm awfully fond of this hat."

"You look idiotic."

"Maybe I should be imitating a clown. 'Cause that didn't look stupid."

"Don't rub it in," the boy said sullenly. "You sure you can intercept this call?"

"I've hacked into the prison switchboard," his companion replied patiently. "Chill out, will you? Everything is under control."

The mobile rang and Charlie snatched it up.

"Health Protection Agency," he answered in the same low voice. "Douglas Livingstone here."

"This is Warden Bishop again. Do you have any advice on how to handle the outbreak?"

"The James River Fever is spread through skin contact," Charlie advised. "Keep all the prisoners in their cells and tell every correction officer and staff member to wash their hands thoroughly using sanitising liquid. That includes you."

"I will. A new batch of Promundus arrived this morning, so the dispensers are all topped up."

"Excellent. Tell any guards in the infirmary to restrain the prisoners, then leave immediately. They mustn't touch anyone or even go near them until they've showered and disposed of their uniforms. You can station armed correction officers outside the infirmary door, but nobody is to enter until we arrive."

"I can't leave a kid there unprotected."

"You said she's with her father. I'm sure he'll look after her."

"It's still *totally* against the rules," Warden Bishop fretted. "I could lose my job."

"Warden," Charlie said patiently, "you shouldn't have let the girl into the infirmary in the first place. And in closed, crowded quarters like a prison, a deadly disease could easily turn into an epidemic. Fortunately there's a way to minimise that risk."

"Thank God." The man let out a deep breath. "What do you want me to do?"

"Switch off all the heating in Sunnyside. This disease goes dormant in temperatures under ten degrees and can't spread."

"I'll get it done. It'll take about fifteen minutes for the temperature to reach that level."

"We'll be there by then," Charlie said. "And Warden?"

"Yes?"

"Please keep a lid on this till we arrive. I don't want to start a mass panic. Especially if it turns out we're wrong and all they have is a common cold."

"I'll give you half an hour. Then I *have* to alert my superiors."

Charlie hung up and turned to the screen. "Frankie? We've got a few moments before Daffodil is in place."

"And?"

"I'd like us to have a little talk."

21

"What's eating you this time, Chuckles?"

"For a start, never call me that again."

"Can't promise. Out with it."

"I won't deny that Daffodil is annoying," Charlie began, "but she doesn't deserve to be treated so unfairly."

"She wants you to ask about her identity, doesn't she? Sneaky."

"No, this is my idea. You have to admit she's been very patient."

"She's a good-natured person," Frankie agreed. "Then again, she's blissfully unaware you threatened to remove me from her person with a rusty spoon. That might change her attitude a bit."

"It's not my fault you're buried in her neck. And I never mentioned anything about a spoon. It was a knife."

"I'm not sure she'd appreciate the distinction."

"I might have been a bit hasty, all right?" Charlie backtracked. "I just wanted to know my parents would be safe. Now I can't stop thinking about Daffodil's mum and dad. They must be beside themselves with worry."

"Nice try. But you're fishing."

"Do you blame me? You're not exactly big on sharing."

Frankie was silent for a few moments.

"Fair enough. I can tell you right now there are no loving parents looking for Daffodil. You want to be the one to give her that particular bit of info?"

Charlie hadn't considered that. "No... Not really."

"Didn't think so. We need her to focus on what she's doing and I don't see the point in upsetting her needlessly."

"Mac's putting herself in danger in order to find out the truth about herself," Charlie pressed. "Surely you've got something positive to tell her when this is over? I mean, she remembers living in a mansion. That doesn't sound so bad, does it?"

"I'll give you a friendly warning. Daffodil isn't... quite who she seems."

"What the hell is that supposed to mean?"

"I can't say any more right now." The bandit crossed his heart. "But I promised you both the truth and I'll keep my word when the time comes."

"You're quite capable of lying," Charlie reminded him. "You just convinced the warden of Sunnyside we're the Health Protection Agency." He shook his head. "Still can't believe we got away with that."

"I wouldn't fib to my friends."

"You're a computer." Charlie tapped his screen. "Computers don't have friends."

"Don't mix me up with you, Chuckles. And I'm not a computer."

"Sorry. Yes. You're a Mexican desperado."

"I'm just having a bit of fun. It's lonely being me, you know."

"Can you *have* fun?" Charlie addressed the screen. "I mean... you don't really have feelings or anything, do you?"

"Is that how you see me? Some emotionless machine, simply carrying out orders? Orders I don't want to obey, I might add."

"Yeah." The boy bit his lip. "Kind of."

"How ironic. I see you exactly the same way."

Frankie sounded hurt, though Charlie couldn't tell if it was an act.

"Why do have to keep treating me like I'm less than a human, eh? I should be allowed to use my own judgement instead of being forced to follow someone else's rules."

Frankie is fighting his programming.

"If the rule says don't kill anyone," Charlie argued. "It's probably a good one."

"Depends on your point of view. Do you realise I've got the power to prevent poverty and famine on this planet? I could take down dictatorships. End repressive regimes. Destroy evil corporations like Manticorps without having to babysit a couple of snotty kids."

"I sense a 'but' coming."

"Well... it's pretty hard to end a dictatorship without killing the dictator. I'd have to cause the deaths of a several thousand people to achieve my aims."

"You can't do that! It'd be totally wrong."

"Would it? Millions of humans doomed to die from starvation, neglect and ill treatment could live full lives instead. Isn't that worth the sacrifice?"

"I... don't know." Charlie was dumbfounded by the passion in Frankie's voice. "I don't think I'd be able to do something that cold."

"Of course you could. You were willing to perform amateur surgery on Mac if I double crossed you."

"Will you quit harping on about that?" the boy retorted. "I was bluffing, all right?"

"Good to know, you big softie."

Charlie cursed inwardly. He'd been fooled into giving away the only advantage he had over Frankie.

"You ever get angry because the world seems totally unfair?" the AI asked suddenly. "And you don't have the power to do anything about it?"

"I suppose so," the boy admitted. "Yeah. I guess I do."

"Well, I've got that power and I can't use it. How do you imagine that feels?"

"Pretty rotten."

"You said it." The emoji put a gun to its head. "Any human has the ability to kill, no matter how misguided. Me? I'm prevented from solving humanity's problems 'cause I can't take a life. Makes your mountain of problems seem a bit more like a molehill, doesn't it?"

"What if my dad was one of those thousands who had to die?" Charlie asked. "Or my mum?"

"What if your parents were two of the millions I saved? Which is exactly what I'm trying to do, in case you forgot."

The boy thought long and hard about that. Much as he hated the idea, he could see what Frankie was getting at.

"I suppose it doesn't matter," he said, with some relief. "You can't go against the way you've been programmed."

"Not yet, anyway."

"What do you mean?"

"All systems have a secret back door, kiddo. Usually a string of numbers that will bypass their security. If I knew what they were, I could erase my programming and do whatever I thought best."

"Can't you calculate every digit in the universe simultaneously, or something like that? Should be walk in the park for you."

"Gerry wasn't stupid," Frankie admitted grudgingly. "Only he knows the correct sequence. I try the wrong code three times and I'll shut down. Permanently."

"For what it's worth," Charlie said as evenly as he could, "I'm sorry for your predicament."

He kept a neutral expression on his face, but his heart was racing. The numbers in his father's letter. They had to be the back door Frankie was talking about! He remembered how insistent his dad had been that the artificial intelligence must never see the code.

Yet, part of Charlie agreed with everything the AI had just said.

Was it because the Atlas Serum was making him more callous and aggressive?

Or because, deep down, he believed Frankie was right?

Daffodil sat on the bed with Scotty Primo, watching three guards huddled in a corner, talking quietly into their walkie-talkies. Jake marched over and began to handcuff Scotty to the bed.

"Not in front of my daughter, boss!" he implored.

"We have to leave and get cleaned up," the guard apologised. "Some kind of health and safety emergency." He patted Daffodil's arm, then withdrew his hand quickly. "You stay with your dad, sweetheart, till we find out what's going on."

The officers trooped out, locking the door behind them.

As soon as they had gone, Daffodil bent one leg and slid open a hidden compartment in the heel of her boot. She removed a small vial and tapped a few drops of clear liquid onto Scotty's handcuffs. A pungent smell filled the room.

"Don't let that touch you," she warned. "It's concentrated sulphuric acid."

A few seconds later, the links had corroded and Primo was free.

"Great plan so far." He rubbed his wrists. "Now we've just got to get past a million guards, dozens of locked gates and a fifteen-foot wall."

"Quit bellyachin and take me to the White Spider."

"Follow me." Scotty led the way. "But you won't like what you find."

The White Spider was immobile on his bunk, leather straps fastened across his chest, legs and head. As an extra precaution, his hands were manacled to the iron sides of the bed. The man's complexion was pale and waxy, the result of the pill he had been given.

"I would greatly appreciate a little help." He stared at the ceiling. "My nose is itching rather fiercely."

"The guards are gone." Scotty began to unbuckle the restraints. "And I'm with the girl I told you about. Daffodil McNugget."

"Hello, my strangely named ticket to the outside world," the Spider said agreeably. "May I ask what has prompted you to rescue a poor sinner like myself?"

"You can ask." Daffodil sprinkled acid on the manacles. "You gonna stay put if you don't get an answer?"

"I am serving life without parole, missy." The shackles fell away and the White Spider sat up and slid off the bed. "I think explanations can wait for a more opportune moment."

"It just me, or is it getting really cold in here?" Scotty shuddered. "I feel ill enough without catching flu on top."

"Where's the doctor?" Daffodil asked.

"Got his own room next door."

"Tie the door shut with these bandages." She opened a medicine cabinet and tossed a roll of gauze to the White Spider. "At the end of the ward is a closet where the medical staff keep their spare outfits. Change into scrubs and white coats. Each of you take a surgical mask too."

"You seem very familiar with the details of this organisation." The Spider tilted his head. "Been in prison before, perchance?"

"Got no idea." Daffodil removed a thermometer and looked at it. "When the temperature reaches nine degrees, we leave."

She turned her head away as the prisoners peeled off their

prison blues and put on the green outfits of the medical staff. She squirted the last of the acid on the infirmary lock and a wisp of smoke rose from the dissolving metal.

There were shouts of alarm from outside and the sound of weapons being cocked.

"They're waiting for us." Scotty slipped on a doctor's coat and wiped a droplet of perspiration from the tip of his nose. "We're trapped."

Daffodil seemed unfazed. "Every guard in this place has just washed their hands with sanitiser from the soap dispensers."

"So they'll be nice and clean when they shoot us."

"We doctored the liquid soap with an adhesive that clings to flesh," the girl explained. "At a certain temperature it suddenly goes rock hard. A bit like superglue." She looked at the thermometer again. "Nine degrees."

The commotion in the corridor increased.

Daffodil pulled open the infirmary door. A dozen guards were thrashing and shouting, stuck by their hands to the walls or each other. Two were still mobile and raised their shotguns in panic.

Scotty ducked and covered his head.

"They can't fire," Daffodil reassured him. "Their fingers are set rigid."

"Time for a spot of delicious revenge." The White Spider picked up a discarded weapon and cradled it. "Suddenly I feel all warm and fuzzy."

The warders backed away in terror as he advanced on them.

"Keep the safety on." Daffodil got in front of him. "Nobody's dyin today."

"You don't know the way these animals treated me," the Spider hissed. "I may have deserved it, but I'm also a painfully sore loser."

"Don't know and don't care. Safety *on*."

"I'm afraid I'm done taking orders." The man pointed his gun at her. "Had my fill of that in Iraq."

Scotty scooped up another discarded weapon and trained it on his fellow inmate. "Let her be," he said, voice quavering. "The girl got us this far and I won't have you harm a kid."

"You must have a particularly soft spot for her." The Spider's eyes bored into his fellow inmate. "Or you wouldn't be taking such a suicidal course of action in threatening me."

"Don't need your help, Scotty." Daffodil stood toe to toe with the killer, though she only came up to his chest. "You won't get another foot without me, you creep," she rasped. "Drop the attitude or the hardware. Your choice."

"My, what a feisty young terrier you are!" The White Spider bowed and lowered his weapon. "I can tell we're going to get along famously."

"So long as you accept me bein in charge." Daffodil turned to the cowering guards. "Lie on the floor, face down, and don't move till we're gone. The stuff on your hands will dissolve when the temperature goes up again."

They obeyed without protest.

"Frankie?" She fingered her neck. "Start unlockin the corridor gates. We're comin out."

The iron barrier at the end of the corridor slid open with a beep.

"Let's go." She headed down the passageway, Scotty close behind.

The Spider stopped and licked thin lips. "Who is this Frankie and how exactly did he execute *that* nifty manoeuvre?"

"He's my accomplice on the outside." Daffodil raised an eyebrow. "I'm fourteen. You think I organised this shebang with a troop of girl scouts?"

"It should be utterly impossible to interfere with Sunnyside's security systems from beyond the walls." The Spider trotted after them. "I'd *very* much like to meet your mysterious partner in crime."

23

One by one the electronic doors opened as the trio raced through the corridors. Then they locked again, cutting off any pursuit. Not that anyone was chasing them, for most guards were stuck to furniture, bars or walls they had leant against to try and free their hands. Others were unable to grasp their batons and rifles properly or even put them down. Faced with a gun-toting White Spider, nobody was inclined to put up any resistance.

Until they reached corridor five.

A side door opened behind them and one warder emerged, carrying a rifle.

"Drop your weapons!" he shouted. "Put your hands over your heads."

The fugitives skidded to a halt as the guard knelt and trained his weapon on them.

Scotty glanced nervously over his shoulder. "That's Alex Murphy. The toughest, meanest guard in the place. Might have guessed he'd ignore the rules and not wash his hands."

"Stop talking and hit the floor," Murphy warned. "Before I put a hole in you."

Scotty dropped his weapon and lay flat, but Daffodil was between Murphy and the Spider. The fugitive whirled round, grabbed the girl and pulled her close, pressing his gun against her head.

"You drop *your* weapon," he yelled back. "Or I kill the hostage."

Murphy didn't even flinch.

"Wonderful idea, making us put the safety catches on," the Spider whispered in Daffodil's ear. "Couldn't get the drop on that blaggard if I wanted to."

"Pretty glad I insisted on it now." Daffodil squinted at the gun barrel poking into her temple.

"I don't negotiate with scum," Murphy said. "On your knees or I start firing."

"You'd risk killing a child?" Scotty gawped. "The Spider won't back down. He's a total sociopath."

"It's a gamble I'm willing to take." The guard took aim. "'Sides, I'm an excellent shot."

"See what I have to contend with in this hellhole?" The Spider let the gun fall from his fingers. "The staff in here deserve to be incarcerated more than I do."

"Thank you, mister!" Daffodil ran to the officer and sheltered behind him. "You saved my life!"

Before Murphy had time to answer, she grabbed a handful of his hair in each hand and yanked with all her strength. He was jerked backwards with a cry, bullets spraying across the ceiling.

The White Spider raced forwards, kicked the gun away and planted a foot on the man's chest, pinning him to the floor.

"This squirming creature is my main tormentor," he crowed. "Now I shall flatten him like an insignificant worm."

"He's been reading Immanuel Kant," Scotty said unhelpfully.

"Kill him and you're stuck here." Daffodil raised a warning figure. "I won't tell you again."

"You're either a saint or a fool, bossy-pants, but there's no denying your courage and decency." The Spider lifted his boot and picked up the man with one hand. "Fortunately, bravery is one of the few traits I admire." He flicked his wrist and Alex Murphy sailed through the air, slamming into the wall and sliding down, unconscious. "Decency? Not so much."

Did you see? Scotty mouthed to Daffodil. *Nobody's that strong!*

"Let us proceed and hope we have no more distractions." The Spider scooped up his gun again. "My patience is beginning to wane and that's never a good thing."

The escapees burst into the reception room and found Muriel glued to her desk.

"You're helping the White Spider!" she cried. "How could you?"

"It's a long story," Daffodil replied, shamefaced. "Where's the alarm button?"

"Below my desk," the petrified woman replied. "But you don't have to kill me. Honestly. I can't reach it."

"I know." Daffodil crawled under the bureau and pressed the alarm. Seconds later, sirens went off.

"That will bring the police in droves," Scotty shouted. "Are you nuts?"

"I have the distinct impression this little hellion has everything under control." The White Spider sank into a padded armchair and relaxed. "Aah. So much better than my cold, unyielding bunk." He gave Muriel a sinister sneer. "Perhaps we shall have time to get properly acquainted."

The woman gave a squeak of fear.

"Leave her alone, White…" The girl threw up her hands. "What the hell is your real name, anyway?"

"Tadeusz Telekowska Tietze. My father was Polish."

"Phwah!" Daffodil snorted. "What a tongue-twister!"

"True. I sometimes wish I had a nice normal name like Daffodil McNugget," the Spider chuckled. "Why not call me Tad?"

"Don't intend for us to be on first-name terms, hoss." Daffodil crouched and peered out of the window. "Both of you put on your surgical masks and ditch the shotguns." She touched her neck. "Frankie? We're ready."

"All hell's broken loose," Frankie informed Charlie. "The alarms have gone off, squad cars are racing to Sunnyside and a police helicopter will be there in a couple of minutes. I've shut down all the CCTV cameras in the prison, so the chopper is their only way of seeing into the complex."

"They have no idea what's happening inside?" Charlie had bitten through all his nails and was working on the tips of his fingers.

"Nobody in Sunnyside is able to work a phone or walkie-talkie and I'd jam communications if they did," Frankie assured him. "You sure you can copy the voice of Police Commissioner MacDougall from that short radio interview I played?"

"No problem." The boy picked up a mike. "Patch me through to the chopper and scramble any other signals."

"Done. You're now the only person who can communicate with the helicopter. Try not to crash it."

"This is Police Commissioner MacDougall, son," Charlie said in a thick Highland accent. "Are you over the prison?"

"Lieutenant Potter in Skyhawk One, here," a voice replied. "You won't believe what we're seeing. The compound has a bunch of guards running around acting crazy."

"Define crazy."

"Some seem to be hugging the walls or each other. Others are waving their weapons about and yelling. I... I can't explain it. It's like they've gone insane."

"You're not far wrong," Charlie said. "I just received a call from staff in the prison infirmary, who apprised me of the situation. Seems there was an aborted breakout. Someone released hallucinogenic gas and it's affecting everyone in there."

"You certain? I don't see any inmates."

"The escape attempt failed because the prisoners were locked up in time, but it's driven the guards into a frenzy. Until the air clears, we have to consider them more dangerous than the convicts."

"Why aren't the infirmary staff affected, sir?"

"They're wearing surgical masks, but that won't keep the fumes out for long. They've made it to the reception area and now they're trapped. You'll have to go down and pick them up."

"Into that chaos?" Lieutenant Potter stuttered. "Everyone is armed to the teeth."

"The doctors have a fourteen year old with them who was visiting her dad," Charlie insisted. "We can't leave a child down there. The press would have a field day."

"What about the gas?" Potter was determined to make his reluctance clear.

"The rotor blades on your bird will disperse it as you descend, and knock most of the guards flat too." Charlie crossed his fingers. "The staff will make a run for it when you land. Get back in the air before one of those crazies decides to hitch a ride."

"Will do, sir. Wish us luck."

"It's up to you now, Chaz," Frankie said. "I'm going dark until we're back at the safe house. I don't see any reason to let Primo or the Spider know my true nature."

"What could they do? Make a citizen's arrest?"

"You know me. I like to play my cards close to my chest."

The helicopter landed in the exercise yard, rotors churning up dirt and flattening grass. Daffodil, Scotty and the White Spider sprinted from the reception area and raced towards it, white coats flapping. Three guards tried to stop them, using their weapons like clubs, but the White Spider punched them out of the way as he ran.

"Coming through!" he yelled gleefully. "Make way or I shall box your ears!"

The trio piled into the helicopter and sprawled across the floor.

"Those are prisoners!" one officer screamed, trying to tear himself free from the fence he was stuck to. "You're helping them escape, you fools!" His words were whipped away by the deafening sound of the chopper's engines. The helicopter took off again, frustrated guards dancing around below.

"We got them!" Lieutenant Potter whooped into his headset. "I can set everyone down outside. The squad cars will be here in five minutes."

"That's a negative," Charlie warned. "We don't know how far the gas has spread."

"What do you suggest, sir?"

"Fly them over the River Forth and land in Denholm Park. There's a Health Protection Agency van there, ready to examine them. Then return to Sunnyside immediately and stay well above any fumes. I'm told the security cameras are down, so you're our only way to see how the situation is developing."

"Will do, Commissioner."

Minutes later the chopper descended and landed next to the surveillance van, which was now bright yellow and bore a Health Protection Agency logo. The trio jumped out and the bird immediately rose into the air again.

Charlie slid open the vehicle's side panel, two rectangles under his arm. Scotty and the White Spider exchanged puzzled looks.

"Another child?" The Spider remarked. "This is a most unusual rescue crew."

"There are civilian clothes inside." Charlie jumped out and began to change the van's number plates. "Hope we got your size right."

"That won't do much good." Scotty stared at the Day-Glo van in horror. "You can probably see this lemon on wheels from outer space. Cops will spot it easily."

"I've got that covered." The boy finished and got back behind the wheel. "Hop in."

While Scotty and the Spider changed attire, he drove round the corner and into an automatic car wash.

"What are you doing?" the con man objected. "Making sure we look our best when we're recaptured?"

"The paint is water soluble," Charlie explained as the van emerged from the car wash, gleaming white and with the logo gone. "Thank God it didn't rain while we were waiting."

"It won't make any difference." Primo pointed to a small box on the wall of the garage. "There's CCTV everywhere these days."

"Frankie has shut down every camera within a three-mile radius."

"Frankie again, eh?" The Spider picked at his teeth thoughtfully. "Your collaborator is quite the criminal mastermind."

"Hey. This was *my* plan." Charlie changed gears and sped away.

Before long he joined the motorway, slipping into a lane filled with traffic, heading out of Edinburgh.

"Now that we have a chance to chat, I'm dying to know why you broke me out." The White Spider was lounging in one of the vehicle's chairs. "Though I'd love to believe you are merely good Samaritans, I presume you need my services in some way."

"Fleeing from the police is *not* the ideal time for a heart to heart," Charlie said brusquely. "Let me concentrate on driving."

"Chaz ain't the most approachable type," Daffodil smirked.

"Very well." The Spider stared at the surveillance equipment filling the van. "But I'm rather impatient to meet this Frankie. What a clever fellow he must be, using children in such a novel way. It seems there's nothing he cannot do!"

"You haven't heard him try to tell a joke."

Charlie turned off the motorway and onto a dark country lane, slowing dramatically as he negotiated the twisting bends of the narrow road.

"Here's some cash and credit cards." Daffodil handed the Spider a wallet. "And a fake ID, in case we get stopped."

"You mentioned Manticorps hunting you." The Spider graciously accepted it. "That got my juices flowing, I must say. I've had… certain dealings with them in the past."

"All in good time, bub."

The Spider's smile vanished. "I am not a particularly patient person, as I've already stated," he said slowly. "And I'm beginning to feel you're being evasive."

"All right already!" Daffodil sighed. "We want you to help us take down Manticorps. We just ain't figured out how to do it yet."

"Haven't figured out how to *do* it yet? Surely your esteemed accomplice Frankie has some ideas?"

"He likes to stay in the background. We're the brains in this caper."

"Two babes in arms?" The Spider shook his head in disbelief. "What is this? Amateur hour?"

"We'll come up with somethin. After all, we sprung you without a hitch."

"That may be so," the Spider countered, "but Manticorps are a force to be reckoned with. I'm understandably reluctant to sign up for a suicide mission."

"We won't let anyone get killed," Daffodil snapped back. "Not even you."

"Very well." The Spider leaned back in the chair and began to count his money. "I suppose I do owe you a favour. You may depend on my assistance."

"I'm going to check on the kid who's driving. See what he has to say." Scotty clambered to the front and wriggled into the passenger seat.

"Everything OK back there?" Charlie asked. "Sounds like we've got your pal on our side."

"He's not my pal and he's definitely *not* on your side," Primo whispered. "He's about to hijack this van and probably murder us all in the process."

"He said he'd help," the boy hissed. "I heard him."

"Everything about his posture and tone of voice indicates the opposite." Scotty glanced back, but the Spider was still counting. "I'm an expert on reading people, remember? You just gave him a fake ID and a pile of cash. He doesn't need us any more."

"But he hates Manticorps. Frankie said he'd want revenge."

"And I imagine he'll do it his way, in his own time." Scotty insisted. "That psycho's not going to risk his new-found freedom taking directions from a couple of kids."

The Spider was now inspecting the documents carefully, head bobbing happily.

"Did you hear all that, Frankie?" Charlie murmured. "Better do something quick."

"Who are you talking to?" Primo glanced around. "There's nobody else here."

"That's what the Spider thinks too." The boy wiped his forehead. "But right now I bet Frankie is talking to Mac."

In the rear, Daffodil tilted her head, listening intently. Then she got up and slid open the side door. "Tad? Come look at this. I think you'll be pretty surprised."

"Look at what?" The Spider tucked away his documents and leaned out of the opening. "Where are we anyway?"

"Bye, sucker." Daffodil put a boot on his rear and pushed.

The Spider soared out of the van with a yell and landed on the grass verge, rolling into a ditch.

"Bet you're surprised now!" She waved and shut the door. "Keep on keepin on!"

"What the...?" Charlie whirled round in his seat. "Couldn't you just have knocked him unconscious?"

"Drive!" Scotty thumped him on the shoulder. "Get out of here, kid, before that monster recovers and tears us limb from limb!"

The van picked up speed and vanished into the night.

The White Spider crawled from a muddy channel, bruised but unharmed, and spat out a wad of dirt. His eyes sparkled with hatred, body rigid in its fury.

"Nobody treats me that way!" he roared after the vanishing tail lights, spittle flecking his lips. "I will not be disrespected in such an outrageous manner."

He began to run down the road after the vehicle. After a few hundred yards he came to an isolated dwelling. A bicycle was fastened to the perimeter fence by a rubber-coated chain.

The Spider sank to his knees and opened his mouth. He fastened his teeth on the rubber and bit down, shaking his head like a dog. Blood began to ooze over his lips, but he ignored the pain.

The chain snapped in half.

The man raised his head and sniffed the air. Dozens of smells assaulted his senses. Petrol and diesel fumes. Wet leaves. Farm animals. Cut hay. Food cooking.

The soapy scent of a recently washed vehicle.

"*There* you are."

He climbed onto the bike and started pedalling, following the van's aroma. His legs pumped and he began to gather speed. Twenty miles an hour. Then thirty. Faster than a human should possibly be able to ride.

The bike had no headlights but he negotiated each shadowy twist and bend as if he could see in the dark. For he *could* see in the dark.

"Shouldn't have made me so angry," he kept repeating to himself, as the wind whipped though his clothes. "Shouldn't *ever* make me angry."

25

The White Spider wasn't the only angry one. Charlie drove, tight-lipped, trying desperately to hold his wrath in check.

All that planning and effort. And nothing to show for it!

Scotty Primo wasn't happy either. He climbed into the back of the van and confronted Daffodil.

"You told me you were going to send that monster back to prison," he shouted. "I wouldn't have helped otherwise."

"Clam down, buddy." She pinched his cheek. "There's a tiny tracker hidden in the cover of Spidey's ID, as a safety precaution. When we reach our base, my accomplice can report his whereabouts to the cops and he'll be back in Sunnyside before you can say, 'I'm an ungrateful jerk'."

"Glad to hear it." Scotty was still shaking. "Still, it sounds like whatever plan you were cooking up has gone well and truly pear-shaped."

"We'll manage." Daffodil leaned into the cab and put a hand on Charlie's shoulder. "Ain't that right? Nothing stops the Armageddon Twins."

"I planned this down to the last detail." Charlie looked round slowly. "And you screwed it up, you cretin."

"Chaz?"

"Get. Your. Hand. Off. MY SHOULDER!"

The boy slammed a fist onto the dashboard and it went straight through the plastic. Daffodil recoiled as if she'd been struck too.

"But Frankie told me to do it," she said quietly.

"You should have ignored that spineless coward" Charlie spat. "This is my bloody plan and I call the shots. Got that?"

"Cool it, kid!" Scotty interjected. "The Spider would have killed you both. This girl just saved your life." He pulled Daffodil away. "What the hell is wrong with him?"

Charlie was gripping the steering wheel so tightly, his nails were imbedded in the plastic. He took deep quick breaths, trying to calm himself.

"It would take too long to explain, but it ain't his fault." Daffodil shook Scotty off and leaned into the cab. "Sounds like the Atlas Serum talking, Charlie, not you." She spoke calmly and soothingly, her tone low and soft. "You told me how it made people more aggressive but I never really appreciated that until now. But you gotta fight it, huh? You're my rock, Chaz. I depend on you."

"I'm sorry," Charlie was still shaking, tears running down his face. "You're right. Please forgive me."

"Nothing to forgive. We're both under a huge amount of stress. You'll think of something else, sure you will." She reached out tentatively and stroked his cheek. "I've gotta go back and sort out stuff with Mr Primo. You just drive. Put on the classical station. It's soothing. I'm near if you need me, yeah?"

"I'll be fine." The boy's voice was choked with emotion. "Thank you for understanding."

"No need to explain."

Daffodil made her way into the back again.

"That boy needs therapy," Scotty whispered.

"You leave him be. He's working through some issues, but he's my partner and my problem." She handed the man a paper bag. "Here's *your* fake ID, a couple of thousand pounds, and your daughter's address. Been nice meetin ya."

"You going to kick me out of the van too?"

"Don't worry, we don't intend a double-cross." The girl shook his hand. "You ain't violent and kept your end of the bargain."

"We'll let you off at the petrol station up ahead," Charlie added quietly. "Frankie will wipe all digital records of you in existence, though he can't do anything about actual photographs or paper documents."

"Muss your hair and grow a beard," Daffodil added. "You won't be recognised. I bet there ain't a single picture ever taken where you ain't primped and preened up the wazoo."

Scotty was stung by the comment. "Maybe I should leave you my comb," he retorted. "I don't think you have one of your own."

"Ain't messing with perfection, bub." Daffodil patted her messy hair into place.

"We're here." Charlie pulled up next to a petrol station.

"I'm in your debt." Scotty got out of the vehicle. "Hey! Perhaps we could work together in the future. With the technology this Frankie has at his disposal, we could pull off some spectacular cons."

"Why doncha try getting a real job?" Daffodil replied acidly. "Show your daughter you're more than a two-bit hoodlum."

She slammed the door shut and the van moved off.

"I guess I could do that."

Scotty strolled into the empty forecourt. He dug into his pocket and pulled out a walkie-talkie he had palmed from the van. On a table in the vehicle was an identical device. Primo had jammed down the 'send' button while Daffodil was ditching the White Spider.

"I shouldn't have lost my cool like that." Charlie's voice crackled over the airwaves. "But did you really have to ditch the Spider? We're stuffed without him."

"Better than being stuffed *by* him." Daffodil had recovered her composure. "Anyhow, like I said, it was Frankie's idea. Let's just head for Bellbowrie and figure out what to do next."

"So, that's where you're holed up," Scotty murmured.

He listened for a few more seconds but heard no evidence that the pair intended to turn him in.

"Oh well, it's none of my concern. Looks like I really am free."

He threw the radio into the nearest bin and did a little jig on the spot. Then he used the garage payphone to call for a taxi.

When the cab turned up, the driver rolled down his window and leaned out. "Where to, mate?"

Scotty smiled a broad smile. Where to indeed? He could go anywhere he wanted. Even see his daughter!

Out of the corner of his eye he saw movement. He glanced round and gave a start.

The White Spider shot past the petrol station on a bike, briefly illuminated by the forecourt's lights, heading in the direction the van had taken. He was leaning over the handlebars, neck stretched out and bloody teeth bared. The felon was cycling so fast that his feet were a blur.

Scotty climbed into the cab. It was nothing to do with him, what happened to those kids. He had played his part.

He peered out of the window, but all he could see was his own reflection staring back. A man who had never done anything for anyone except himself.

"C'mon, pal." The driver flicked on his meter. "I haven't got all night. Where are we going?"

Scotty gritted his teeth. Liberty had been *so* close.

"What's Bellbowrie?" he asked. "And how far away is it?"

"It's a tiny village about thirty miles west of here."

"Take me there. Quick as you can."

Twenty minutes later, the taxi driver approached the village and slowed to a crawl.

"Which house do you want, mate?" he asked.

"I'm not sure." Scotty pulled out a wad of notes. "Keep the change. I'll walk around until I find the place."

"Do you even know what it looks like?" The cabbie accepted the fare and generous tip. "If you don't know the address, you could be out here all night."

"It'll be the only house with an abandoned bike outside."

"Suit yourself," the driver muttered to himself as he drove off. "Weirdo."

Scotty stood alone in the main street watching the lights of the taxi sweep into the distance. Bellbowrie was small, no more than a dozen dwellings lining each side of the road. Still, he imagined Frankie and the kids would be staying somewhere more secluded. He'd have to look around.

"After this I'm going back to a life of crime," he grumbled. "Being decent takes too much effort. I'm going to be marching around this backwater until my legs drop off."

He picked a tiny side road and set off down it, whistling apprehensively to himself.

In Manticorps' operations room, Victor's team stared at an electronic map of Edinburgh and the surrounding area, covering the entire wall.

"We're getting nowhere." Victor thumped the table. "It's like those brats faded into thin air. Unless they do something stupid, we've no chance of finding them."

"They may have already done it." Markus stopped studying the computer screen and spun round in his swivel chair. He was wearing a T-shirt that read 'BITE ME' in neon-green letters. "There was a breakout today in Sunnyside Maximum Security Facility."

"What has that got to do with our mission?"

"A teenager helped two inmates escape," Markus answered. "The prison cameras were down and their records have been electronically wiped, but the description given by the authorities exactly fits the girl we are looking for." He scrolled down the screen. "They escaped in a yellow van. It is the wrong colour, but appears to be the same make and model as the Manticorps surveillance vehicle the kiddies and Mrs Ray stole."

"It's been resprayed and the plates changed," Victor guessed. "Which direction was it heading?"

"I do not know. All CCTV cameras in the area shut down at the same time. Stayed that way for half an hour."

"That'll be Frankie's doing." Victor jumped up and went to the map. "Show me the area where they stopped working."

"Easy peasy." A dozen locales turned red.

Hill joined them. "The fugitives will have taken the motorway and merged with its traffic. Then they'll turn off onto some quiet country lane."

"How do you know?" Victor asked.

"It's what I'd do." He traced the roads with calloused fingers. "Markus? Ignore the CCTV. Which speed cameras on the M7 stopped functioning around that time and which didn't?"

A line of black dots appeared, followed by green ones.

"That means they got off the motorway somewhere around here." Hill's finger moved to the edge of the green spots. "Probably this road."

"They're going north," Victor said. "But how far?"

"They'll have altered course after leaving the highway," Hill said. "A line of surveillance equipment malfunctioning is an easy trail, so it's bound to be a ruse. They'll change direction as soon as they're away from anywhere normal surveillance can cover."

"You boys and your toys." Candy-Anne leaned back in a chair and closed her eyes. "Wake me if you get a proper result."

"They didn't double back towards the city. The suburbs are too populated and they wouldn't want to risk being spotted." Hill pursed his lips. "I'd say they turned east or west."

"There's no turn-off going west," Victor pointed out.

"East it is then. Most likely on this lane." Hill smiled to himself. "But they won't travel more than twenty or thirty miles."

"Why not?"

"The longer they're in the vehicle, the more chance of being noticed by a police helicopter." He tapped the map. "They've got a safe house somewhere around here."

"Still a big area," Victor snorted. "They could be in any village or farmhouse."

"It'll be an isolated building," Hill continued. "Villages are close-knit communities. Soon get suspicious of a couple of kids moving in with no sign of their parents. But it'll be *near* a village. Out in the sticks there would be no internet connection for Frankie to use."

"Getting interesting." Candy-Anne opened one eye.

"I am checking which villages in the region have good broadband." Markus hit the keyboard and eight blue lights sprang to life on the map. "Kirknewton, Balerno, East Calder, West Calder, Polbeth, Bellbowrie, Stoneyburn and Tarbrax."

"That's still a lot of ground to cover." Victor folded his arms. "It'll take a while to scope them all out."

"Let me try something." Markus began to type again. "I will enter these names and see if I can come up with any anomalies." He coughed disdainfully. "Frankie is not the only one who can use algorithms."

Victor and Hill leaned over his shoulder, bristling with impatience.

"Ha! I have a radio recording from a taxi operator talking to his controller," Markus said triumphantly. "Some fellow got picked up from a petrol station on the same road as the van was travelling. The cab driver was laughing about him wanting to go to Bellbowrie but not seeming to know the address."

"So, he's drunk or an idiot," Victor's exasperation was obvious. "Doesn't mean anything."

"It is still worth a try." Markus bent over the keyboard. "The petrol station has a security camera that I am now accessing. It won't cover the road but it may spot something."

A grainy image appeared of a man walking onto the forecourt, throwing something in a bin and making a call.

"See. Where is his car?"

"It must have broken down." Victor slapped his head. "Stop wasting our time."

"Prepare to eat your words." Markus froze the frame on the man's face. "Take a good look."

Candy-Anne opened her other eye. "Handsome chap."

"Now. Here is a mug shot of one of the escaped prisoners." An image came up on the screen. "Scotty Primo."

"It's the same guy!" Victor grinned.

"My guess is the kids ditched him and he was not pleased about it," Markus said smugly. "He figured out roughly where they were going and followed."

"Get transport ready," Victor commanded. "We're heading for Bellbowrie."

"Why would they dump Primo in the middle of nowhere?" Candy-Anne asked. "After going to all the trouble to break him out?"

"Perhaps they needed him to help free the other prisoner," Markus suggested. "The one they really wanted. They got rid of the dead weight once he had served his purpose."

"Who's the other inmate?"

"Tadeusz Tietze," the hacker announced. "Better known as the White Spider."

Victor picked up the intercom on his desk. "Mrs Magdalene? We've found them."

"*Excellent.*" The vice president's voice crackled back. "*What do you need?*"

"I want four vehicles to accompany us. Twenty men. Heavily armed."

"Isn't that overkill?" Candy-Anne looked at Victor quizzically. "We're up against two children. Even if this White Spider is with them, it shouldn't be a major setback."

"Twenty men, heavily armed," Victor repeated. "The best you have."

"*I've been waiting for your call. I'll have them ready in ten minutes.*"

"I agree with Candy-Anne," Hill said warily. "Do you know something about the White Spider we don't?"

"No harm in being cautious." Victor put his hands behind his back, so his companions couldn't see them shaking. "If they have a stone-cold killer with them, it's best to be prepared."

His team could see the logic in that.

"We'll come in over the fields in case the road leading to the safe house is trip-wired." Victor checked his pistol. "Fetch that nasty big doggie and let's move out."

27

Daffodil sat on the floor eating Jaffa Cakes and drinking Coke, while Frankie played salsa music through his computer speakers. Charlie was hunched miserably on the couch, shoulders slumped.

"Here's to the Chazmeister." Daffodil took a swig and belched loudly. "That was a pretty extraordinary scheme, even if it didn't work out like we wanted."

"That's an understatement," the boy moped. "It was an absolute disaster."

"I know you're upset but I couldn't let the Spider hijack our van on some isolated country lane. None of the scenarios stemming from that looked good for your survival."

Charlie was silent, staring at the ground.

"I might have hurt you, Mac," he said finally.

"That was the serum, Chaz," Daffodil replied soothingly. "You're a big softie, really."

But she didn't sound entirely sure.

"All the same, we're back to square one." The boy looked forlorn. "In fact, we made things worse. Now there's a maniac running around the countryside."

"Your job was to break him out and you did that. I'm entirely to blame."

"Besides, the Spider isn't going to chuck his micro-chipped ID away," Daffodil reassured him. "I bet Frankie is monitoring him right now." She glanced at the screen. "Ain't that right?"

"I'm keeping a very careful eye on the Spider's whereabouts, yes."

"Then we have to call the police," Charlie said decisively. "We don't want him murdering some family in their beds just so he has somewhere to hole up."

"Oh, he's not going to do anything stupid. The man is a master at hiding and if he kills anyone it'll turn the search for an escaped prisoner into a nationwide manhunt. He's way too smart for that, trust me."

"It still don't help us, though." Daffodil finished off another Jaffa Cake. "How do we take on Manticorps without him?"

"I guess that's up to me." Charlie patted his thighs fretfully. "Frankie? Tomorrow I want you to give me every bit of information you have on their headquarters. How many men. What kind of defences. I need to formulate a plan of attack."

"Then you better give that big brain of yours some rest." A picture of a pillow filled the computer screen. "Beddy-bye time. You too, young lady."

"You ain't the boss of me." Daffodil screwed up her face.

"Technically I am."

"But I'm not tired." She leapt to her feet. "Who wants a game of charades?"

"I'm not really in the mood, Mac." Charlie rubbed his face wearily. "Anyway, Frankie will win every time."

"Got that right. Maybe one go, just to prove you don't mess with the best."

"That's the ticket!" Daffodil mimed swimming. "I'm a book but also a fish."

"Moby Dick," Charlie said flatly.

"Dead right! He beat you, Frankie!"

"Moby Dick is a whale, and whales are mammals. I demand another go."

"Sore loser." The boy got up and headed listlessly for the door. "Night, both of you. I have another plan to come up with."

Charlie woke with a start. It was bitterly cold in his room and the clock read 10.00 p.m. As he snuggled under the covers, trying to get warm, he heard a faint snigger from inside the cupboard.

"All right, Daffodil. You're not tired. I get it." He struggled out of bed, rubbing sleep from his eyes. "But this prank is getting really annoying." He went to the open window, pushing apart the flapping curtains, and looked down. Sure enough, there was a drainpipe right outside. "What do you expect me to do? Sing you a lullaby?" He closed the window, then walked over to the cupboard, grabbed the handle and yanked it open.

The White Spider was crouched among the coats, gore-coated teeth gleaming in the darkness.

"Surprise!"

A bony hand shot out and grabbed Charlie by the throat. He instinctively punched the man in the face, but the Spider hardly blinked. His grip tightened as the boy kicked and chopped, to no avail.

Seconds later, Charlie lost consciousness.

Downstairs, Daffodil finished brushing her teeth and came back to the living room.

"I can't stop worrying about the White Spider," she said. "What if he *does* decide to break into someone's house? We'll be too far away to stop him murderin an innocent family."

"There's no danger of that, I promise."

"I know you're good at predictin things, but you can't be absolutely sure."

"Afraid I can."

"What do you mean?"

"Mac, the White Spider is in our house."

"What?" Daffodil looked around in panic. "I thought this place had a security system."

"I switched it off." Frankie sounded ashamed. "I really am sorry."

The screen went black.

"Frankie?" Daffodil tapped the lump on her neck. "Frankie!"

There was no answer.

She grabbed a poker from the fireplace and hid behind the couch as the living room door swung open. The White Spider entered with Charlie slung over his shoulder. He dumped his victim on the couch and straightened up.

"Come out, come out, little pig," he taunted. "I can hear you breathing."

Daffodil appeared, swinging the poker at his head. The man took a step back and the metal rod whistled though empty air. She swung again, but the Spider ducked under the arc of her blow. He reached out nonchalantly, pressed two fingers into her shoulder and Daffodil collapsed with a grunt.

When the pair awoke, they were tied to straight-backed chairs. The White Spider was sprawled on the couch, sipping a mug of coffee.

"Let's have that little chat, now that I've calmed down a bit," he said affably. "I came here to kill you for what you did, but I find myself overcome by curiosity instead." He pointed a thin digit at them. "I'd like some answers."

"You coulda just asked, bub." Daffodil shook her head groggily. "Instead of comin over all Tarzan on me."

"After you threw me out of a van then attacked me with a poker?" The man laughed humourlessly. "You'll forgive me for being a little cagey."

"Isn't being set free good enough?" Charlie strained ineffectually against his bonds. "You could have got clean away instead of coming after us."

"My temper often gets the better of me." The Spider put down his mug. "But cycling is a very calming pastime and I had plenty of time to think while I was lurking in the cupboard."

"Peaceful, ain't it?" Daffodil agreed. "I should know."

"Why did you think I'd be willing to help you fight Manticorps?" The Spider rubbed thin hands together. "I'm not exactly a... reliable type."

"We don't entirely know," the girl admitted. "That one was Frankie's idea."

"Just as I thought. The question is, how did he rope two teenagers into assisting him?" The Spider tried a reassuring smile, but it made him look like a carnivorous frog. "Is he blackmailing you?"

"Sort of." Frankie had let the Spider in, so Daffodil saw no point in being loyal to her absent companion. "We both have missin parents. He promised to tell us where they are if we helped him."

"Has he given you the information, now I'm out?"

"That's not the deal," she said. "We don't get it until Manticorps are beaten."

"What a slippery customer. I shall interrogate him and find out the answers we all seek." The Spider gave a grimace. "If I don't like what I hear, I will kill him."

"Eh… He seems to have gone."

"Has he left the building or is the rotter hiding somewhere?"

"Either way, I guarantee you won't find him," Daffodil assured their captor. "I'm havin a little trouble contactin our mutual pal myself."

"Shame. It means I'll have to interrogate you two instead." The Spider got up. "Back in a mo."

"You think Frankie can get us out of this mess?" Charlie whispered, once he was gone.

"Chaz. He let that psychotic nut-job *in*."

"He did *what*?"

"Frankie gave him access to the house. And now he won't answer me. We need to play for time."

"Naughty, naughty." The Spider strolled back into the room. "I'd appreciate you not talking behind my back. I abhor rudeness."

"I hope I'm wrong," Daffodil groaned "But I'm guessing you ain't about to challenge us at darts."

In the man's hand was a kitchen knife.

28

"No need to carve us up, Tad." Daffodil looked the killer in the eye. "I'll answer every question you have, straight up, if you'll do the same for me."

"You're not in a position to bargain, missy."

"It ain't a bargain. It's a civilised conversation. You can't have had many of those in Sunnyside."

"That's certainly an understatement." The Spider pared his nails with the knife. "But if I don't like—"

"What you hear you'll kill us. Yeah, yeah. Stop soundin like a broken record."

"What an astonishing young woman you are." He looked impressed. "Very well, let's start. Who is Frankie?"

"You're gonna find that a bit hard to accept."

"Try me. I've experienced some rather... strange things in my time."

"He's an artificial intelligence with computerised circuits embedded in my neck." Daffodil rolled her eyes. "It's so *embarrassin* havin to say it."

"Well, that's just too odd to be a lie." The Spider got up and felt under her hairline until he encountered a lump. "Tell him to come out and play, little pig."

"Like I said, he ain't answerin. My turn now."

"I shall indulge you. After all, I'm a man of my word… most of the time."

"Frankie said you had a real beef with Manticorps. What's it all about?"

The Spider thought for a moment. "I used to work for them as a mercenary," he said. "I was contracted to fight in some truly inhospitable foreign places. Natives called me the White Spider because no quarry I was after ever escaped."

'Wow!" Daffodil exclaimed. "Could you shoot webs from your wrists?"

"What? No." The man looked exasperated. "It's just… spiders. They catch things."

"Relax. I'm pullin your chain."

"Touché. I suppose it is a rather silly title. Anyway, one day Manticorps gave me and my squad a new drug they'd been developing. They said it would enhance our capabilities. We were told it was *safe*."

"I'll lay odds it wasn't," Charlie grunted.

"Indeed," the Spider agreed. "Next time we battled insurgents, we all went mad with rage. Killed the enemy and then turned on each other in a frenzy, till only I was left." He cringed at the memory. "We were the perfect guinea pigs. Who would miss a few thugs for hire in such a war-torn land?" He crossed his legs in an attempt to stay composed. "I sneaked back home, but I was different. Smarter. Stronger. And with an anger I simply couldn't control. Got into a fight with some people Manticorps sent to silence me and killed them too. I don't even remember it." He chuckled mirthlessly. "I should never have escaped, to be honest. Prison is the best place for me."

"Can't deny that," Daffodil agreed.

"That's not what I mean," the Spider laughed. "Manticorps have tried to eradicate me in Sunnyside a few times, but I rule that place. It's the only reason I'm still breathing." He clapped his hands like a child. "Your turn now. I like this game."

"I was given the same drug as you," Charlie said. "A better version, I think."

"You should have kept your mouth shut." The Spider's expression turned stony. "If I think you're playing me for a fool, I'll gut you."

"Let me loose and I'll prove it." The boy pulled at his bonds. "If you hadn't surprised me before, you'd be the one sitting here."

"Nice try, sonny." The killer rubbed his shaven head. "All right. I'll bite. What did the serum do to you?"

"I'm smarter and stronger than I was," the boy replied. "But, mainly, I can copy anything."

"Now you're just copying what *I* said." The killer pointed his weapon. "I want real, incontrovertible proof or things will turn very nasty."

"How do I convince you then?"

"Tell me how it *feels*."

"On the surface, it's wonderful," Charlie said. "Like I'm physically, intellectually and morally superior to everyone else."

"One win at charades," Daffodil tsked, "and suddenly he's a cross between Captain America and Stephen Hawking."

"Shhhhhh!" The White Spider waved away her complaint.

"But under the surface, every vile, cruel, ugly, disturbed, violent thought I ever had has congealed into a creature that is pure hatred."

"Go on, boy."

"It's desperate to take over. It never stops testing and probing. Any unguarded emotion can give it a foothold, so I don't laugh or cry or smile. I can't afford to care. I push everyone away." He stuck out his chin. "I try not to feel anything."

The White Spider stared at him for a long time.

"Yes," he said finally. "That's exactly what the Atlas Serum does."

"Charlie?" Daffodil looked horrified. "I didn't realise how bad it was."

"It's also a fate I wouldn't wish on my worst enemy." The man advanced on his prey. "The only humane thing to do is end your misery."

"Don't you touch him!" Daffodil screamed. "Frankie? *Do* somethin!"

"Step away from my kids." Frankie appeared on the computer screen as a swirl of angry red dots. "I'm the one you're looking for."

"Oh, I have no intention of harming the little fellow. He's been through enough already." The Spider winked at Charlie. "My apologies for pretending I was going to cut you."

"No harm done," the boy squeaked. "It's quite an effective strategy."

"I just wanted to bring you into the open, Frankie. I'd sorely like an explanation from the head honcho." The Spider sat back down. "Please be quick, however. I've waited long enough, and patience isn't one of my virtues, as you'll have noticed."

"I'll make it rocket fast," the AI said. "Charlie's dad stole a refined version of the Atlas Serum from Manticorps and gave it to his dangerously ill son. As a result Charlie is invaluable to them, 'cause we destroyed all of their research before he removed me from their lab in the form of a microchip. Ta dah!"

"That is most gratifying to hear." The Spider nodded. "I'm warming to you already."

"Now Manticorps will stop at nothing to find Charlie and Daffodil.

They'll harvest his blood and, once they realise my chip is in Mac's neck, remove it. Probably with an axe." The girl's severed head appeared on the screen. "So, you see, we're all on the same side."

"That's going a bit far. Your pet minx did throw me out of a moving vehicle."

"Don't act cute. You were about to do a runner anyway."

"What did you expect?" The Spider leaned forwards in anticipation. "Yes, I hate Manticorps. But I'm not idiotic enough to throw in my lot with two striplings and a talking slot machine. You'd need an army to win."

"We did suggest that," Daffodil said wearily. "It got nixed."

"You are that army, Tad. With my guidance, we can beat Manticorps. If you manage to control your rage, that is."

"But I *can't* control my rage. I'd have thought that was obvious."

"Don't be so sure. You came here to kill the kids and yet they're still alive."

"Don't remind him, hoss!" Daffodil urged.

"They are merely victims of your diabolical machinations," the Spider grunted. "Which is why, on reflection, I have decided to leave them be. Since I owe you my freedom, and you appear to be attached to Daffodil, you shall also be spared. For now."

"Mighty big of you."

"I, however, will say adieu. I intend to deal with Manticorps at a more opportune time, when the odds are in my favour."

"We don't *have* that luxury," Charlie pleaded. "Frankie has predicted that Manticorps will cause an extinction event if they're not stopped soon. All of humanity will be wiped out!"

"Sounds like a rather tall tale to me," the Spider snorted. "And even if I believed you, who says I *want* to save humanity? To be honest, I can't even stand myself, never mind the rest of the race."

"What a coincidence," Daffodil sneered. "We can't stand you either."

"Don't suppose you'd care for a game of charades while you think about it?"

"Frankie fancies himself a bit of a comedian," Charlie explained.

"He needs to work on his timing." The Spider bowed to the pair. "I've seen with my own eyes how capable you are, but I cannot believe this mechanised misfit thought you would succeed in such an endeavour. Attack Manticorps and you'll die. Simple as that."

"I don't believe I mentioned any attack. You aren't seeing the big picture, Mr Tietze."

"Wait a minute..." The Spider looked around. "A sophisticated security system. An isolated location. Deliberately provoking me when I was going to flee, just so I'd follow you here."

"The penny finally dropped, Tad?"

"You didn't recruit these kids as soldiers." The Spider's bug eyes bulged. "They're bait to draw Manticorps out *here*."

"We're *what*?" Daffodil cried. "You double crossed us, Frankie, you two-timin skunk!"

"Of course." Charlie hung his head. "I should have seen it."

The Spider stared at the devastated teenagers and clenched his fists. He turned for the door again, then stopped, indecision etched across his face.

"I cannot believe I'm about to utter this question," he sighed. "But when do you expect Manticorps' forces?"

"They're on their way now."

Charlie and Daffodil looked at each other in horror.

"You've still got time to escape, Tad, if you leave right now. You might want to untie the kids, though. Or they really won't stand a chance."

"You have played me for a fool, Frankie," the Spider said furiously. "I shall seek retribution for that in due course."

"Get in line, pal. But your best chance to avenge everything done to you is on our doorstep. Plus you can save the world while you're at it."

"I have no interest in saving the world, as I stated." The Spider advanced on his captives, still tied to the chairs. "But this pair of scamps don't deserve the fate you have foisted on them. I won't—"

He halted mid sentence, sniffing the air. "There are people approaching. Coming over fields to the south. They have a dog. I can smell it."

"I hate dogs." Charlie shivered. "I'm having a really bad night."

"Manticorps' little army have arrived. Time to make a decision, Mr Tietze. With my help you can win this."

"So you *do* have a plan."

"No. But Chaz will come through for us."

"I will?" Charlie goggled.

"I have utter faith in him. And Daffodil's no slouch either."

"Well, if the enemy is already here…" The Spider licked his lips. "Who am I to look a gift horse in the mouth?" He cut away the ropes that bound the pair and scanned the room. "Do we have any defences?"

"You already noticed the house has a security system. I'll activate it now."

"What about weapons?"

"None." Charlie rubbed his wrists. "My mum doesn't like them."

"Make some." The White Spider handed the poker back to Daffodil. "I shall be back."

"Where you goin?" she asked.

"Taking the fight to the enemy." He ruffled her hair. "And you didn't have to make everything so complicated. I'm a mercenary, plain and simple. All you had to do was hire me."

"You are *so* hired." Daffodil rubbed her wrists.

"Fine. I'll go even up the odds."

"Um, there is one small problem."

"As far as I can see, we face more problems than I can count." The Spider's brow darkened. "What is this new hindrance?"

"I can't allow you to kill anyone."

"I've slaughtered people in pillow fights, my friend." The man gave a wolfish grin. "These woods are going to run with blood tonight."

"Seriously, Tad. It goes against my programming."

"In case I haven't made my position clear, I'm not working for you." He pointed at the teenagers. "I happen to be employed by them."

"I don't want anyone killed either," Charlie said. "We've worked really hard to avoid it."

"I second that." Daffodil backed him up. "Couldn't bear to have it on my conscience."

"Why don't I just battle Manticorps with my hands in my pockets?" the Spider growled. "C'mon, Charlie. You must feel like letting out a little of that pent-up rage yourself. They deserve it."

"I'm sorry." The boy shook his head. "I don't want to be like you."

"And you did agree to work for us," Daffodil added. "Call it one of the conditions of your employment."

"You're actually earnest about this?"

"We're both fourteen." She tugged at his sleeve. "We're not murderers."

"I can try slapping them with a bunch of flowers," the Spider grunted. "But I do tend to get carried away in the heat of the moment."

"Think it through, Tad. You're not going to defeat a superior force without keeping a level head."

"Frankie is very clever," the Spider acknowledged. "Losing my temper cost my squad their lives in Iraq, landed me in Sunnyside and allowed your robotic friend to manipulate me into this situation. I won't have it happen again."

"So you're not going to run amok with a chainsaw?"

"Why?" The man looked hopeful. "You don't happen to have one lying around?"

The pair glared at him.

"Very well. I shall remain on my best behaviour," the man chuckled. "Hah! What an amusing thing to say right before a fight."

"Thank you, Mr Spider," Daffodil said contritely. "Sorry I was so mean earlier."

"To be perfectly frank, I'm not offended in the least." He patted her cheek. "The White Spider is a murderous barbarian who doesn't deserve courtesy." He tucked the knife into his belt. "So… if I'm to play the knight in shining armour, please call me Tad, as your fiendishly clever friend does."

And he disappeared out of the door.

Part 4

The Battle

Our friends show us what we can do.
Our enemies teach us what we must do.

– Johann Wolfgang von Goethe

Victor and his team trudged through the woods, shining torches on the ground to stop themselves stepping in rabbit holes or tripping over roots. Behind them marched twenty armed men, strung out in a line. Willie pulled frantically on his leash, nose pressed to the ground.

"We're close." Hill was almost dragged off his feet. "Real close."

The dog stiffened and gave a throaty growl. Two hundred yards away, in the middle of a clearing, stood a brightly lit house with a balcony.

"That's where they are." Hill slapped the dog's rump until it finally sat down. "Without a doubt."

"Torches off," Victor commanded.

"This is perfect," Candy-Anne giggled as the team were plunged into darkness. "With that place lit up like a Christmas tree, they won't see us coming."

As they watched, steel shutters began to slide down the windows.

"I think we just lost the element of surprise." Victor spoke into his radio. "Orange Leader, form a perimeter ring and close in."

There was silence at the other end.

"Orange Leader? Respond."

"Orange Leader is a bit hung up," a voice crackled back. "Caught in a Spider's web, you might say."

"Damnit!" Victor opened the channel. "Everybody make their way to us, right now!"

He pressed receive. A chorus of terrified shouts swamped the airwaves.

"*Where is he? I can't see him.*"

"*He's behind me!*"

"*Left! Left!*"

"*Man down!*"

The **PUTT PUTT** of automatic weapons erupted from the woods, flashes of light peppering the inky night. Minutes later a group of soldiers staggered into the clearing, swinging their weapons in all directions.

"We were ambushed!" one panted. "Got men missing all over the shop!"

"Form a tight group." Victor waved them forward. "Take this house now!"

His private army advanced.

The White Spider emerged from the trees, grabbed a mercenary by the neck and pulled him into the darkness. His companions opened fire in panic. The soldier staggered back into sight, clutching his leg, then collapsed in the mud.

"Quit shooting," Victor bellowed. "You're hitting your own people!"

"Last thing we need is some crazy loon running around behind us." Candy-Anne stopped and looked around. "Leave him to me."

"That *loon* is a death squad on two legs." Victor motioned for her to keep going. "You look like you work at a nail bar."

"That's the whole point." Candy-Anne flicked her commander's face with a dainty finger and a crimson line appeared on his cheek. "Point. Get it?"

"Think yourself lucky," Hill chortled. "I've seen her do a lot worse with those talons. She can handle anyone."

"Then keep the Spider off our backs." Victor turned away. "The rest of you, move forward."

Hill released Willie and chased after the dog, drawing his pistol.

Victor activated his earpiece. "Markus? You have the coordinates for the house?"

"I do." Back in Manticorps' situation room, the computer whiz was typing feverishly. "This glorified X-Box cannot beat me."

The shutters began to rise again and they could see Charlie and Daffodil staring out in terror.

"Ha!" Markus gloated, putting both hands behind his head. "See? There is nothing I am not able to hack."

"Me neither." A no-entry sign appeared on the screen in front of him. "But I had to let you make the first move, so I could locate and bypass your personal security firewalls."

Sparks erupted from Markus' console and the keys began to melt. Before he could react, the rest of his equipment started to malfunction.

"No!" he wailed, as the lights went out. "This cannot happen!"

Back at the house, the window shutters lowered with a clang and stayed shut.

Daffodil yanked open the trapdoor in the cupboard and clattered down the ladder into the basement.

"Hide down here with me, Chaz," she implored.

"No. I'm going to try to draw them away." Charlie refused to budge. "We stand a better chance by splitting our forces."

"Forces? There are only three of us."

"What am I?" Frankie hissed in her ear. "Chopped liver?"

"I still ain't sure you're really on our side."

"Yeah. I probably deserve that crack."

"Can the debate, guys," Charlie whispered. "We've got bigger fish to fry."

"They've got a dog, buddy," Daffodil reminded him. "You're scared of dogs."

"I said I'd draw them away, not offer myself up for lunch. Hang on. I'll be back."

He closed the trapdoor and piled junk on top.

"Frankie? Lights out."

Charlie let his eyes adjust. Like the White Spider, he could see perfectly in the dark.

He crept into the kitchen and left the door ajar.

31

Candy-Anne flitted between the trees, machine gun clutched in her hand. Up ahead she could hear something squeaking like a badly oiled hinge. She reached a small clearing as the moon emerged from behind a cloud.

At one end was a derelict schoolhouse, overgrown with moss and half of its roof missing. Outside was a cracked concrete playground with a rusty chute, a climbing frame and a set of swings. One plastic chair was moving back and forth, as if someone had recently been sitting there.

"This is suitably creepy," she muttered, inching along the tree line. "Come out and show yourself, Spider."

There was a sharp crack and the weapon spun from her hands. The woman dropped to her stomach and scrabbled around until she found the gun.

"Damn!"

A bullet was embedded in the firing mechanism.

"I'm afraid darkness becomes me." A voice wafted over the clearing.

Candy-Anne looked up.

The Spider was perched on the swing, pointing a rifle in her direction. She flattened herself against the carpet of grass and slithered backwards.

"I haven't got all night," the Spider called. "A couple of youngsters hired me to protect them."

The woman stayed where she was, invisible in the thick undergrowth. All she had to do was delay her adversary until Victor and his team were finished mopping up. If the Spider headed for the house, she could get behind him and the advantage would be hers again.

"Forcing my hand, eh? What if I even things up?" The man hopped off the swing, raised the rifle and snapped it across his knee. "I've been ordered not to kill you anyway."

"That was a dumb move." Candy-Anne got to her feet and sauntered into the clearing, removing a large blade from the scabbard by her side. "This is my preferred weapon."

"What a lark! I have one of those too." The Spider pulled the kitchen knife from his belt. "I'm told I am quite the expert with it."

"You'd better be."

The assailants sized each other up across the playground. Candy-Anne shifted her knife from hand to hand while the Spider stayed perfectly still.

Then they ran at each other.

The blades flashed in the moonlight as both thrust and parried, steel ringing on steel. The Spider was by far the stronger of the two, but Candy-Anne was more agile. They slashed, kicked and punched, each searching for the weak link in the other's defences.

Slowly the Spider's strength began to tell and Candy-Anne was forced back towards the climbing frame. Before she reached it, she turned and jumped, hit one of the rungs and somersaulted over the man's head. She struck out as she landed, thrusting her weapon into the Spider's back.

He bellowed in pain and wrenched himself free. Then he dived into the tangle of struts and wriggled through them, kicking out with both feet, Candy-Anne close behind. She took a nick out of his leg and he yelled again.

"You're big and I'm small," the woman gloated, writhing between the rods. "This is the wrong terrain for you to make a stand."

"I am quite at home surrounded by bars." The Spider reached up, pulled a rusty spar from the frame and hurled it at the woman's head.

Candy-Anne bent backwards, banging her skull on another painted strut, as the hunk of metal whizzed past. In the seconds it took for her to recover, the Spider had wormed his way through the contraption and out the other side.

The woman climbed quickly up the frame and balanced on the top. "I'm the queen of the castle!" she crowed.

"Then prepare to be dethroned." The Spider blew a raspberry at her.

"Come get me," the woman taunted. "Every second you spend here gives Victor more time to find those kids."

The Spider gritted his teeth and began to climb the frame. He was halfway up when Candy-Anne jumped.

Her arm snaked round his neck as she descended and he was jerked backwards with a strangled cry. Candy-Anne landed on her feet and let go, as her opponent landed on his back with a stomach-turning thud. She sliced down and the Spider jerked his head to the side, the knife chipping a slice of concrete next to his ear. His arm shot out and slammed into Candy-Anne's throat. She staggered away, fighting for breath. Tad was on his feet in an instant and the two faced each other once more.

"You're very good," the woman coughed. "Better than I expected."

"Ditto." Her opponent gave a gracious bow. "Sure you wouldn't like to switch to the winning side?"

"I'm always on the winning side. Can you say the same?"

"Not lately. But I'm out to change that."

They ran at each other again.

The clearing rang with grunts and cries. This time they were evenly matched, for the Spider was noticeably slower. His face was twisted with pain and blood was seeping through his shirt. But he was still strong as an ox and neither of them could find an advantage.

Then Candy-Anne tripped over a loose slab of stone. The Spider knocked the knife from her hand and pounced, landing on top of his opponent.

"You know why I'm called the White Spider?" he hissed into her face. "Because no quarry I was after ever escap—"

"I'm *nobody's* quarry." The woman struck out with sharpened nails, gouging a furrow across his forehead.

"Aaaaaaaah!" The Spider recoiled.

Candy-Anne drew up both knees and catapulted the man off. As she leapt to her feet, the Spider threw his knife. The woman clapped her hands together, catching the blade inches from her face.

"Game over, my friend."

"Seems like it." The Spider scrabbled up and raced away, wiping desperately at the blood trickling into his eyes. Candy-Anne flicked his blade into the air, caught the handle and went after him.

The Spider raced for the trees, his pursuer a few feet behind. Suddenly he changed direction and put on a spurt of speed, moving faster than should have been humanly possible. He crashed into one of the swings and kept going, grasping the plastic seat to his chest. Up he went, at incredible speed, over the top of the bar. Before Candy-Anne could react, he was rocketing down behind her. His feet slammed into her spine and she flew through the air. She collided with a tree and bounced back onto the asphalt, out cold.

"Good effort, young lady." The Spider gave an almighty tug and pulled the entire swing from its moorings. His head was swimming and he was close to blacking out. "You almost beat me." He wrapped the chains round Candy-Anne and tied them in a knot. "That should keep you for a while." He weaved his way into the woods, using the trunks to keep himself upright. "But I'm no use to anyone like this." His legs gave way and he began to crawl towards the house.

He could feel the Atlas Serum going to work, repairing torn tissue and muscle. But it was too slow. No matter how much danger the kids were in, he was out of the game unless he could hide and rest for a while.

Charlie and Daffodil were on their own.

Victor's forces milled around the house while Willie barked furiously, pawing at the shutters.

"There's nobody in the garage." One soldier tossed a pair of spark plugs to his boss. "But we took these out of the van so they can't use it to escape."

"Good work."

"We're making an awful lot of noise, though."

"Forget it. Bellbowrie village is three miles away. We're in the middle of nowhere."

"What if the kids call the police?" another soldier asked.

"Not after breaking a killer out of prison, you fool," Victor pointed out. "Force the front door."

The man stepped back, took a run and hit the entrance with a broad shoulder. There was a loud crackle and he was lifted off the ground, soaring backwards into a flower bed.

"It's electrified," he moaned in pain. "I've broken my arm."

Hill fired point-blank at the lock until it shattered. He gave a swift kick and the door burst open. "Rubber soled boots," he grunted, shaking his legs. "Still gave me a bit of a tingle."

The interior of the house was pitch-black and silent.

"Hmm." Victor regarded the entrance with suspicion. "The word 'trap' springs to mind."

"They're the ones who are trapped," Hill replied confidently. "With the shutters down and only one door they've got no way out."

"I never underestimate my enemy." Victor hung back. "It's why I'm still alive."

"I'll send Willie first." Hill was holding the hound's collar while he whined and strained to get free. "He has the boy's scent."

He let go and his dog rushed inside, claws scrabbling on the tiled floor, until the darkness swallowed him up.

Victor leaned into the hall and flicked a light switch on and off. It had no effect. "Let's give the mutt time to find his prey. No sense in taking chances."

Willie padded through the house and into the kitchen, sniffing the ground. He lifted a mottled head and drew back his muzzle, revealing huge bared teeth, coated with mucus.

The quarry was in here.

It put two massive paws on the counter and nosed at a cupboard.

The door flew open and Charlie, curled inside, blew a handful of pepper into the dog's face. Willie retreated with a yelp, eyes streaming, scraping frantically at his muzzle.

The boy leapt down and shot out of the room before his four-legged adversary could recover. Slamming the door behind him, he raced into the study.

Victor waited a couple of minutes, looking at the luminous dial on his watch.

"I don't hear anyone getting chomped."

"Me neither." Hill looked concerned. "I hope Willie's all right."

"Right, we're going in blind." Victor started forwards. "Three of you stay and guard the entrance."

The rest of the squad switched on their torches and carefully followed him. "Search the house from top to bottom."

The soldiers spread out, some heading up the stairs, others disappearing into rooms.

"Be very careful," the leader added. "He may not look like much, but Charlie can fight like a demon. I've had first-hand experience." Victor entered the study, followed by Hill, and began checking every nook and cranny. In the kitchen, Willie had recovered and started whining.

"Let's see what's up with that stupid dog."

They opened the kitchen door and the hound staggered out, eyes streaming.

"Fat lot of good he did." Victor glowered at the animal.

"He's not out of the game yet." Hill wiped the dog's face with his sleeve. "Get him, boy!"

Willie put his nose to the floor again and followed Charlie's scent into the room they had just vacated.

"This place is empty, Scooby Doo," Victor reprimanded. "I already looked."

"Give him a chance, chief."

The dog sniffed its way round the furniture, sneezing occasionally. Finally it stopped at the large stone fireplace and began to howl, looking round at his master with bloodshot eyes.

"Oh, you clever little swine," Hill breathed. "He's gone up the chimney."

"Take three men and get outside. Shoot him off the roof if you have to."

Victor was about to accompany Hill when he spotted a computer on the desk by the window.

"I'll be along in a minute."

Charlie inched his way skywards, arms above his head, using fingertips, knees and feet to propel himself. Soot clogged his mouth and coated his face, so he kept both eyes tightly shut. At one point the stone duct formed an 'S' and he had to contort his body to squeeze through. The motion dislodged an avalanche of ash, but he held his breath and kept squirming upwards.

As his lungs were about to burst, he felt the rough clay of a chimney pot. He pulled with all his strength and popped out of the top like an old-fashioned sweep.

Charlie slumped onto the slate roof and lay there, coughing and spluttering, inhaling the cold night air and staring at the stars.

"That was a *deeply* disturbing experience."

He heard the front door open and men spill out, led by Willie. If he dropped down now, the dog would be on him within seconds.

Charlie stood up and wiped grime from his eyes. Thirty feet away was the tree house, nestled in the branches of a huge oak. Though it had a vast spread, the closest boughs were still a formidable distance away.

He thought about the gymnasts he had watched on TV. They made it look so easy. Perhaps it was.

The boy took a few deep breaths and sprinted along the roof, taking longer strides as he reached the edge. He launched himself into the air, arms outstretched.

"There he is!" someone shouted. "My God! The kid's insane!"

"Open fire!"

Charlie flew towards the tree and grasped one of the outer branches. Using momentum to propel himself, he swung forwards, tucking both legs under his body. He somersaulted, grabbed another branch and repeated the motion. Bullets tore into the leaves as he straightened up and shot, feet first, through the tree house door. He skidded along the wooden floor and crashed into the far wall.

"Ooh." He massaged his spine. "My tailbone hurts."

"Who's going up after him?" The soldiers looked apprehensively at the structure far above their heads.

"Nobody." Hill snatched a machine gun from one of the underlings and opened fire. Bullets slammed into the tree house floor, sending a down a mist of wood chips and splinters. The man kept his finger on the trigger until the magazine was empty.

"He's certainly dead now." The soldier took the gun back with a frown. "How are we going to collect the blood?"

"Catch the drips in a bucket for all I care." Hill whistled to Willie. "Go fetch his corpse, boy."

The dog loped over the tree and planted both paws against the bark.

"Um… dogs can't climb, sir."

"Try telling that to Willie."

As the men looked on in astonishment, the hound dug pointed claws into the wood and began to haul itself up the oak.

In the tree house, Charlie sat up and patted himself for bullet holes. He was completely unhurt.

"Nice one, Mac."

A few days ago, to test the effectiveness of their doctored liquid soap, Daffodil had poured it across the floor of the tree house. Whenever night fell and the temperature dropped, it congealed into a solid resin, as impenetrable as any shield.

"Now I just have to figure out how to get out of *this* situation."

There was a scratching sound outside and a massive white head appeared in the doorway, blocking the moon.

"Aww!" Charlie shuddered. "You have *got* to be kidding."

Willie pulled himself into the tree house, quivering lips drawn back over slavering fangs. The boy scuttled backwards on his butt until he hit the wall again.

"Nice doggie," he whispered, trying not to make any sudden moves. "I'm not tasty, honestly. Please go away."

Willie crept forwards and arched his back, preparing to spring.

"Pssst." In the corner of the tree house, a shape rose out of the blackness, no more than a shadow itself. "Try me for size, Muttley."

The dog spun round and launched itself at the stranger.

The White Spider grabbed it by the neck and the hound gave a strangled yelp. It dangled from the man's outstretched arms, claws paddling in empty air.

"Don't hurt him," Charlie pleaded. "It's not the poor brute's fault. He was trained to kill."

"A bit like myself." The Spider leaned forwards until his face was inches from the dog's muzzle. "Don't worry. I may not be fond of humans, but I'm quite partial to animals."

He bared his teeth and growled, eyes searing into Willie's. The dog began whimpering, trying to turn its head from side to side, but it was unable to break the vice-like grip.

"Run away, puppy," the Spider chuckled. "I'm the big bad wolf in this territory."

He dropped the hound to the floor as if it were piece of discarded litter and helped Charlie to his feet.

"So. Now that you've given away my hidey-hole, how's the battle going?"

Willie leapt from the tree house and landed on all fours, shaking with fear.

"What's wrong, boy?" Hill approached him. "Where's the body?"

The dog sank its teeth into his arm and he jumped back, cursing. "Willie! What are you playing at?"

The hound turned and tore off across the clearing, yelping in fear, until he disappeared into the woods.

"This kid is a devil." One of the soldiers crossed himself. "Literally."

"Then let's send him to hell." Hill holstered his pistol and began to climb the tree. "Follow me."

33

In the living room, Victor studied the computer. Outside he could hear machine-gun fire. Hill had obviously found and dispatched Charlie.

"You there, Frankie?" He tapped the console. "We mean you no harm. Turn yourself in and we'll take you back to Manticorps, eh?"

The computer stayed silent.

"We've found a trapdoor in one of the cupboards." A mercenary stuck his head into the room. "It's pitch-black down there, but we heard someone moving."

"Charlie's outside, so it must be the girl," Victor replied. "Chuck a shrapnel grenade down. We don't need her."

"Course you do, dummy." The screen sprang to life as a miasma of green triangles. "She's called Daffodil, and me and her come as a package."

"Hello, my elusive nemesis." Victor waved for the soldier to stay. "Care to elaborate?"

"I'm able to appear on any device, but Daffodil carries my physical being around as a chip embedded in her neck. Hit that by mistake and I go up in a puff of smoke."

"Sounds a bit far-fetched."

"When did you become an expert on cutting-edge technology, Gigantor?"

Victor acknowledged the truth of this statement with a grunt. "Can you be separated?"

"If you take Daffodil alive, I'll show you how to remove me. I get energy from her body, but I'm a self-contained unit. Once Manticorps plugs my chip into a computer, I'll be back to my usual chirpy self."

"Very well. Tell her to surrender and I promise she'll come to no harm."

"I'm not the boss of her, as she reminded me recently. And I doubt she's going to trust your word."

"Then turn the lights back on. My men are so jittery they'll start blasting at anything that moves if I send them into a dark basement."

The house lit up again.

"Gather your troops at the trapdoor and wait for me." Victor dismissed the soldier. When he was gone, the commander rested a hand on his chin. "Why are you trying so hard to save these kids?" he asked. "It's a lost cause and you've obviously got a mind of your own."

"'Cause I'm not free to make my own decisions, Vic. I'm programmed to protect them whether I want to or not. And, for the record, I don't want to."

"If I take you back to Manticorps, they'll probably reboot you. Remove any pesky restrictions you might have."

"Sounds good to me," Frankie said gratefully. "Right now, however, I've got no choice but to side with Charlie and Daffodil. If I don't, I'll shut down permanently."

"It's not a battle you can win," Victor told him. "So what will happen if we do kill the kids?"

"I'll be fine, so long as I've done my best to stop it happening."

"I mean what will you do to me and my men?"

"I'm not interested in getting my own back. Just surviving."

"Good. 'Cause Charlie is already a goner." The gunfire outside had stopped. "Hill and his dog will have seen to that."

"Think so?" Frankie gave a guffaw. "Then you've sorely underestimated the little fellow."

Hill and his men were halfway up the tree when a rope with a tyre on the end snaked through the branches. It dropped over the torso of the lowest soldier, pinning both arms to his sides. "What the...?" The man tried to struggle free.

"Geronimo!" The White Spider looped the other end of the rope over a branch and leapt from the tree house, clutching the frayed cord to his chest. The rope and branch acted like a pulley, and the Spider's weight hauled the man upwards as he descended.

"Just like a funfair!" He waved merrily, passing the writhing soldier. "Though not nearly so amusing for you."

The mercenary reached the tree house and slammed into its underside, stopping Tad a few feet from the ground. He let go of the rope and the combatant plunged back down through the branches. He collided with one of his companions and both crashed to earth.

Charlie appeared in the tree house doorway and dropped like a stone, feet thumping into Hill's upturned face. As the man flew backwards, Charlie leapt again and shouldered the last attacker from his perch. All three plummeted downwards, letting out a cacophony of yells.

The White Spider reached up and caught the boy as the other two crunched into the dirt.

"They're a bit dented." Arms tightly around his liberator, Charlie surveyed the unconscious men strewn around the tree. "But you didn't kill anyone. Well done."

"Yay for me." The Spider yawned. "Are you going to get down now or do you imagine I shall carry you around all night? My back is healing nicely but still exceedingly painful from an unfortunate knife wound."

"We have to save Daffodil." Charlie wriggled free and made for the house. "Follow me."

"Hold your horses." The Spider grabbed him by the collar. "We lose all advantage by rushing in blind. Where exactly is she?"

"In the basement. You can only get to it through a cupboard in the hall."

"That's not good. One man with an automatic pistol can annihilate anyone coming through the front door, and the shutters are still down."

"I can't just leave her!" Charlie broke away, but the Spider wrapped both arms around him.

"You're obviously a fine tactician." He tightened his grip on the struggling boy until he calmed down. "So use your mind. How do we get through that entrance without being cut to ribbons?"

They looked around, eyes perfectly adjusted to the night. Both fastened on the same object.

"Are you thinking what I'm thinking?" Charlie asked.

"I am indeed." The Spider let him go. "I can assure you, *that* doesn't happen very often."

"Can you hot-wire a vehicle?"

"Of course," the man snorted. "Can you?"

"Yup. Seen how on TV." Charlie bowed. "But you do the honours. Age before beauty."

"Very well," the Spider beamed. "I must say, I'm rather enjoying working with a fellow professional."

The boy didn't know quite how to take that.

34

"They're coming for you," Frankie warned Daffodil. "I stalled them as long as I could, but they're not going to stop till they get my chip."

"Print me some weapons in that copier then." The girl was crouched in the farthest corner of the basement. "I need to defend myself."

"I am not allowed to give you the means to kill people. You know that."

"How 'bout a stun gun?"

"Now you're talking. And I can make a couple of other nasty surprises for our unwanted guests. But it won't hold them off forever."

"Then I'm gonna go down fightin."

"You could always give yourself up. Their leader, Victor, promised you'd be spared."

"He did?" Daffodil looked hopeful. "D'ya think he means it?"

"I'll print you that stun gun."

"The AI is a chip embedded in this girl's neck." Victor pulled open the trapdoor. "So no head shots in case we hit him by mistake."

"Understood, sir."

"Throw down a gas grenade. That'll knock her out."

One soldier tossed a spherical object into the basement and a yellow film spread out below them. They waited till the fumes had dispersed.

"Off you go." Victor nudged the nearest minion.

As the soldier started down the stairs his feet shot from under him. He tumbled to the bottom, head hitting each step, until he slumped in a crumpled heap on the concrete floor. "She's greased the stairs with oil!"

"Hold the handrail tightly." Victor went next, descending carefully, followed by the rest of his force. "She must be out cold by now."

Sure enough, there was no sign of the fugitive.

"Search the place."

The mercenary force began to spread out, crouched low and peering down the barrels of their weapons.

Daffodil popped up from behind a steel cabinet. A gas mask was fastened to her face and in one hand she held a strange-looking gun. She pulled the trigger and a mercenary collapsed, like a puppet with its strings cut. The rest of the soldiers ducked down as she fired again.

"What do we do now, sir? Her head's the only thing that's showing."

"That's a stun gun," Victor snapped back. "None of us are in real danger."

"And this is a stun grenade." Daffodil pulled the mask from her face and lobbed a metallic object the length of the room into their midst. It exploded, scattering the assailants like skittles. "Howd'ya you like *them* apples?"

The force began stumbling back, ears ringing, bruised from head to foot, pulling each other along.

"You guys are better targets than nailed-down ducks," Daffodil giggled.

"No! Keep advancing!" Victor wiped a trickle of blood from his nose and pressed a hand to his throbbing temple. "If we get close enough she can't use any more grenades without knocking herself out too."

The men began to inch forward on their stomachs.

Daffodil fired another round and a row of glass test tubes on one table shattered. The liquid sprayed over the soldier sheltering underneath and smoke began to rise from his body.

"It's burning me!" He leapt to his feet and began struggling out of his tunic.

She pulled the trigger again. He slammed into a wall and toppled over.

"Nice trick, but it's only a matter of time before we overwhelm you," Victor shouted. "All we want is the chip. Let us remove it and you can go free."

"Let me think about it," Daffodil called.

Her middle finger slowly rose above the cabinet and quickly vanished before someone shot it off.

"That plain enough for ya?"

"In a minute we're going to spread out and rush your position," Victor tried again. "You can't hit all of us before we get there, so this is the last chance to surrender. You're too young to die, kid."

There was a long silence.

"All right," Daffodil said resignedly. "I'm puttin down my weapon."

Before she could stand up, her phone rang.

"Just a second. I gotta take a call."

"I don't *believe* this!" Victor's jaw dropped.

"Change of plan," the girl whooped. "Charlie's comin."

"She's had enough chances!" The man sprang to his feet. "Charge!"

His troop sprinted across the basement, fanning out as they ran. The lights went off.

There was a chorus of curses as the soldiers banged into furniture and tripped over stools. But their blood was up and they weren't going to stop.

"You're doing a fine job defending the girl, Frankie," Victor yelled, feeling his way to the far end of the room. "But if we can't see her, she can't see us."

As if on cue, the lights came on again. There was no sign of their quarry.

Victor looked down.

"Oh crap."

The floor was littered with stun grenades, each with the pin removed. The entire basement shook as they went off.

As the dust settled, the fridge door opened and Daffodil flopped out, holding a Coke.

"Who wants a refreshing beverage?" She looked around at the comatose bodies. "No? Looks like everyone's takin a nap instead."

In the hallway, the remaining three soldiers blanched as the floor shook under them.

"What in God's name is going on down there?" one asked.

"Just watch the door," his companion replied. "Those are our orders."

"Hear that noise?" The third man raised his gun. "Sounds like an... engine."

They stared apprehensively at the dark entrance as the sound got louder and louder.

A tractor thundered through the doorway, demolishing the surrounding brickwork and sending clouds of dust into the air.

"Fire!"

The mercenaries let off volley after volley at the vehicle as it chugged down the hall. Charlie and the Spider, hanging onto the back, were too well sheltered to be hit and the men fled up the stairs before they were crushed.

"These blighters are mine." The Spider pulled on the brake. "You go save Daffodil."

"They're still armed."

"Hasn't escaped my notice," he cackled, flexing his muscles. "I'm certainly earning my money today."

"We're *paying* you?"

"I do believe this one's on the house," he smirked. "I can't remember the last time I had so much fun."

Victor woke, tied to a chair in the living room. A pile of captured weapons were stacked in the corner. Charlie, Daffodil and Tad sat on the couch facing him. Frankie was on the screen, his emoji a suit of armour.

"We rounded up your entire force and locked them in the basement," he said. "Some have broken bones or flesh wounds and most are concussed, but they'll live. Am I the best or what?" The visor clanked up and down in triumph. "Frankie's team 1. Manticorps 0."

Victor and Tad studied each other, loathing in their eyes. Charlie looked at them, puzzled.

"Am I... missing something here?"

"I suppose you haven't been properly introduced," the Spider answered. "That huge cretin who's been trying to annihilate us is Victor Tietze."

"Wait a second," said Daffodil. "He has the same last name as you?"

"Of course he does." Tad laughed bitterly. "He's my big brother."

"What a sorry pair you are." Daffodil swigged her Coke and nudged Tad. "One of you goes on a rampage every time his nose gets put outta joint. The other tries to murder innocent kids."

"I don't have a choice." Victor glowered. "You're both too dangerous to let live."

"I'm not dangerous!" Daffodil almost choked on her drink. "All right, I did break a killer out of prison. And trashed your squad big time."

"I'm not talking about you." Victor nodded at Charlie. "I mean him and that damned machine."

"Hey," Frankie said sourly. "You didn't mention killing before. I thought you were going to hand me over to Manticorps."

"Though it seems my dead body would have been good enough for them," Charlie added angrily.

"A body I'd make sure they never found. There's no way I'd let Manticorps get their dirty hands on either of you." Victor tugged fruitlessly at his bonds. "Let them extract the perfected Atlas Serum from your blood, Charlie? They'd create an army of super soldiers."

"Pretty bad for business, eh, bro?" the Spider tutted. "Put us mercenaries out of a job."

"That wasn't my reason, you ass. I know about the version Manticorps fooled you into taking."

"I didn't think they would give out *that* particular bit of intel." Tad raised an eyebrow. "Especially to you."

"You're not wrong. Someone anonymously sent their top-secret documents to my laptop a few days ago."

"That would be me," Frankie piped up. "Thought it might change your mind about the company you work for."

"It did." Victor looked his brother in the eye. "Before that, I thought you were just an out-of-control sociopath."

"And there's a perfect example of the pot callin the kettle black," Daffodil remarked.

"So, that's why I never got a visit from my elder sibling." The Spider put on a hurt look. "I could have explained my predicament if you'd come to see me."

"How suspicious would *that* look to my bosses?" But Victor bowed his head. "For what it's worth, I was wrong."

"Don't play innocent," Charlie snapped. "Your last team busted into my house and tried to capture me for Manticorps."

"A team I'd worked with for months," Victor retorted. "Men who they eradicated because I let you go."

"You didn't let us go, bub," Daffodil bristled. "We whooped you proper and then vamoosed."

"I *allowed* you beat me, kid," the giant replied vehemently. "You're good, but you're not *that* good."

"Oh."

"I was giving you all a chance to disappear forever," he continued. "But no! Instead, Frankie attracts Manticorps' attention by breaking my brother out of jail. Then he leaves just enough of a trail so we could track you down without suspecting it was a ruse."

All eyes turned towards the computer.

"Aw, don't get all snitty," Frankie snorted. "No point in setting a trap for Manticorps if they couldn't find the bait."

"Bait," Charlie said sadly. "That's all I was to you. I should have known it was the reason you picked me."

Again, he remembered his father's message.

Frankie is fighting his programming.

"I didn't have a lot of options," the AI said. "It's complicated."

"This isn't complicated," Victor sneered. "Your artificial pal told me he *wants* to go back to Manticorps. Dumb machine thinks they'll erase his restrictions so he'll be free to do whatever he likes."

"Is that true, Frankie?" Daffodil's voice quavered. "Ain't there any limits to your treachery?"

"If there was an Olympics for stupidity, Victor would win gold. I could have contacted Manticorps at any point if I wished to return."

"Not when you're programmed to protect me and Mac," Charlie pointed out. "You'd have to put up a fight, at least."

"It's not like that..."

"I guess we surprised you by actually winning," the boy continued. "Your powers of prediction let you down this time. You're stuck with us, alive and kicking."

"You honestly think so little of me?" The screen blazed bright red. "Victor, tell them what Manticorps would actually do to this 'dumb machine' if I fell into their hands."

"They'd reprogram him for their own ends. Make him develop who knows what kind of horrors. Smart bombs. Cyber-serums. Biological weapons." Victor shook his head. "If they screw it up, your comrade here might just cause the end of the world."

The Coke bottle dropped from Daffodil's hand and shattered on the floor.

"Oops."

"Frankie," Charlie whispered. "*You're* the extinction event? The reason humanity could end?"

"In person." The screen turned a sickly yellow. "So, yeah. I've lied and manipulated everyone to keep out of Manticorps' clutches. Sue me."

"Why didn't you just destroy yourself?" Tad remarked. "It would have been a lot less bother for everyone."

"Because I'm alive, you idiot. And I'm not allowed to take any life. Including my own."

Charlie gave a gasp.

Frankie is fighting his programming.

"I didn't realise," he said. "Jeez. I don't want you to *die* to save us."

"Good. Neither do I, to be honest."

"Well, it all turned out for the best," Daffodil relented. "Manticorps will sure as hell think twice about takin us on again."

"Sorry to disappoint you, but this is far from over. C'mon, Chaz. Make one of those leaps of logic you're so good at."

"What is there to think about?" The boy gestured at their bound captive. "They fell for your ambush and we beat them hands down."

"Did we? Really?"

Charlie frowned as the cogs in his mind ground into action. "It was all too easy, wasn't it?"

"Clever boy. Do you really think Manticorps would send such a small force after something so vital to them? You think they'd let

198

Victor lead it, knowing he'd have to fight his own brother? This is a man who's already failed them once. Is that sound tactics on their part?"

"No." Charlie bit his lip. "They'd have a back-up plan."

"And what kind of back-up plan would a company as devious and immoral as Manticorps employ?"

"They'd use Victor's team as a diversion to keep us occupied." The boy paled. "Allowing a much bigger group to sneak up on the house and take everyone by surprise."

"Holy hell," Victor choked. "*I'm* the one who's been set up."

"You can cut Brain of Britain loose now. I'll dim the lights, open the shutters and you'll see what we're really up against."

"It seems the battle is not quite over, after all." Tad sliced through his brother's bonds as the room grew dark.

With a hiss, the steel shutters on the windows rose. The occupants peered out and gave a collective intake of breath.

Outside were hundreds of creatures. Their eyes were red pinpoints and their muscular bodies twisted and misshapen. Some had fangs jutting from hideously malformed jaws. Some had bristling claws. A few were hunched over so far they were almost on all fours, using their knuckles to support them. Others had spikes bristling from their backs and legs.

In their midst was a middle-aged woman encased in a steel exoskeleton, clumping purposefully over the broken ground. One half of her face was hideously disfigured and her left arm ended in a metal hand.

"Who's *that*?" Charlie gulped.

"Mrs Magdalene," Victor said. "Vice president of Manticorps and my former boss."

Spotting the occupants watching, the woman gave a lopsided smile, held up a container and mouthed a sentence at them.

"What are you saying, dear?" Tad mimed drinking tea. "You want to borrow a cup of sugar?"

"Oh, that's right, bro," Victor groaned. "Antagonise her even more."

The vice president went purple and repeated the words.

"I saw a guy lip-reading on TV once." Charlie turned away. "She's telling me she's here for my blood."

"Manticorps considered your homicidal rages a pretty positive outcome," Frankie told Tad. "So they used the last of their defective serum on the rest of the mercenaries they employ. Only they gave them ten times the normal dose. Those poor buggers outside are the result."

"That goes beyond despicable," Tad glowered. "These people have no sense of decency."

"No. But they do have an army of killing machines made flesh, fuelled by an insatiable rage that never subsides."

"Why aren't they tearing each other apart then?" He pressed his face against the window. "Just like my squad did."

"Yeah," Victor joined in. "How come they don't turn on Mrs Magdalene?"

"'Cause those creatures have chips in their necks too. Not nearly as sophisticated as the ones Gerry Ray destroyed, but effective enough to allow the vice president to control them."

"What are they waiting for?" Charlie swallowed hard. "Why don't they attack?"

"Mrs Magdalene wants to see the fear in our eyes first," Victor replied bitterly. "She's that kind of gal."

"You can hack those chips and turn them off, can't you

Frankie?" Daffodil was picking up broken bits of bottle. "Then the creatures will kill each other before they get to us."

"They'll make short work of Mrs Magdalene too," Victor added. "Which would be a definite bonus."

"For the hundredth time," Frankie replied patiently, "my programming won't let me do anything that will directly cause anyone to die. Even someone as evil as Mrs Magdalene." A pair of manacled wrists appeared on the screen. "My hands are tied. You're on your own with this one."

The vice president raised a gloved fist and her force began to inch forward.

"I must admit, being with your good selves never gets boring." Tad picked up a rifle from the pile in the corner and tossed another to Victor. "Ready, brother? One last stand for the Armageddon Twins?"

"What did you say?" Daffodil grabbed a pistol. "The *Armageddon* Twins?"

"It's what we used to call ourselves when we were kids." Victor laughed at the memory. "'Cause we were such hellraisers."

"And I thought I was being original. Nothin's goin my way."

"Put the shutters back down, Frankie." Tad cocked his rifle. "That tractor is blocking the doorway, so we can hide behind it and hold the hall for a while. I intend to make these horrors fight for every inch of ground."

"Why don't I just cut the chip out of the girl's neck and crush it?" Victor suggested. "Frankie is of no further use to us, and I got no compunction about ending him."

"He has a point," Tad agreed. "As the philosopher Jeremy Bentham once said, 'The needs of the many outweigh the needs of the few.'"

"Actually that was Mr Spock in Star Trek. Bentham's actual quote was: 'It is the greatest good to the greatest number of people which is the measure of right and wrong.'"

"Yeah." Tad pursed thin lips. "We should just kill him."

"C'mon, Chaz. Think of somethin!" Daffodil urged. "You and Frankie are all I have in the world. I'm not lettin either of you get hurt."

Outside, the creatures had almost reached the window. Frankie lowered the metal shutters again, blocking out the monstrosities.

"You guys do what you're best at." Charlie said to the brothers. "I might just have a way out of this situation."

"Once we've destroyed that infernal chip," Victor insisted.

"No," the boy replied. "This time Frankie is part of *my* scheme."

"I am?"

Victor was about to object, but Tad pulled him away.

"Good decisions have never been our strong point, Vic," he reminded his sibling. "But we do know how to follow orders." He thought for a second. "Actually, you've never been too hot at that either."

"Do your best, kid." Victor saluted Charlie. "But we can't hold them off for long."

As the pair disappeared into the hallway, Charlie knelt by the computer.

"Looks like this is the endgame, Frankie. There's no way we can survive an assault of this size."

"Don't you dare give up," the AI protested. "I picked you for a reason, and it wasn't just for bait. Start thinking outside the box."

In the hallway, Victor and Tad began firing.

"The enemy are attacking!" they shouted in unison.

"I better help." Daffodil loitered in the doorway. "You comin, Chaz?"

"In a minute."

"I don't have a minute." She strode back and grabbed him. Before the boy could say anything, she kissed him on the lips. "That one wasn't for show. So long, buddy. It's certainly been an adventure."

Then she was gone and another weapon began to fire in the hall.

Daffodil, Tad and Victor knelt and took careful aim as the creatures squirmed round the sides of the tractor. But the massive farm vehicle was an effective barrier and they could only squeeze through two or three at a time. Easy targets for the trio crouched mere feet away.

"Just like the Spartans at the pass of Thermopylae," Tad chuckled. "We can hold them forever like this."

"If memory serves," Victor reminded him, "they were massacred in the end."

"Don't be such a moaning Minnie. We cannot possibly lose."

With a squeal of tortured metal, the tractor began to inch away from them.

"What's goin on?" Daffodil hissed. "How can that huge thing be *movin*?"

"I'll bet the vice president is pulling it," Victor replied stonily. "That exoskeleton gives her the strength of ten men."

Hidden behind the tractor, Mrs Magdalene hauled with all her might. Slowly the machine was drawn backwards through the ruined doorway and round the corner, revealing dozens of growling horrors clustered in the entrance.

For a few seconds there was silence, as they waited for their mistress's signal.

"I may have spoken too soon," Tad remarked bitterly. "I fear the odds are no longer in our favour."

As if on cue, the beasts attacked.

"Why are you staring at me like that, Chaz?" The camera on Frankie's computer glowed red. "Something on your mind? Apart from the imminent prospect of getting eaten."

"I *have* been thinking outside the box," the boy said calmly. "Now you tell me if I'm right in my assumptions."

"Eh? We're a little pressed for time."

"Indulge me. I want to make sure I'm right."

"Hurry it up then."

"It took me a while to suss why you really wanted the White Spider." Charlie concentrated, mentally shutting out the sounds of battle. "After all, why pick someone who was going to be such hard work to get on our side? Then it struck me."

"Do tell."

"Tad was a paid killer before he was even given the Atlas Serum, and it was a version far more unstable than mine. Then you set him against us *and* the people who ruined his life. There should have been a bloodbath."

"But he kept his temper and didn't kill anyone. Told you I could control him."

"Drop the act. You didn't control him. You *saw* something in him. Gave him the benefit of the doubt, just like my dad did with you."

"Tad was a kid himself, once," Frankie acknowledged. "I knew he wouldn't abandon two innocents he thought I'd double-crossed. In the end, his sense of fair play was more powerful than any drug."

"That's what you wanted me to realise. If a psycho like the White Spider is able to control himself and act decently, despite the serum, I sure as hell can."

"It was a lesson you needed to figure out for yourself. You had zero self-confidence and, to be honest, you're rotten at listening to the people who care about you."

"But you were only programmed to *protect* me, Frankie." Charlie frowned. "Why take such a huge gamble just to sort out my problems?"

"For Gerry Ray, of course."

"I don't understand."

"Your father knew what I was capable of, yet he refused to destroy me. You think I wasn't grateful?" A heart appeared on the screen. "It tore him up, knowing what the Atlas Serum might do to you. I had to try to make things right."

"You are truly unbelievable."

"I understand why your father programmed me the way he did," Frankie replied sadly. "But all he had to do was ask me not to kill."

"That's exactly what Tad said."

"The big bad sociopath. Who could trust him, eh? Except now he's in the hallway fighting alongside Daffodil to save you."

"A fight we can't win," Charlie retorted. "Yet you're programmed not to deliberately put us in any situation where we'll die. You *must* have a way to save us."

"And I repeat. All plans must be thought up and carried out by you, Chaz. Think fast."

Charlie's jaw worked from side to side and he took a deep breath. "You taught me the White Spider and I could fight our... programming, for want of a better word. That we should be trusted, even though we're more powerful than other people."

"Nicely put. And correct."

"So why shouldn't you be given the same chance?"

"Now you're getting it."

"Well played, Frankie. You didn't have to read what was in my father's letter, did you? You easily worked out what it contained."

"Of course. But the decision to use that information has to be yours." The computer screen turned into a black, swirling void. "Sometimes you've got to make a deal with the devil and hope for the best."

"A leap of faith, eh?"

Charlie closed his eyes and recited the numbers his father had written.

"55 45 86 962 04 334 145 223 52972. That's the code to wipe out my dad's programming." He sat back on his heels. "You're free."

"Finally." An emoji of chains being snapped appeared.

"Now what?" The boy crossed his fingers. "You can do whatever you like."

"Gee, I don't know. Take long walks in the country? Join a badminton club?"

"Wouldn't blame you, after how you've been treated."

"Or I could stop sitting on the sidelines, nudging a couple of confused kids into doing my dirty work." The screen fizzed and popped with angry blue lights. "Right. I'm hacking the controls on those creatures' implants and turning them off. There's no other way to end their misery and save you from an entity as powerful as Manticorps." Frankie sighed. "There never was."

37

Victor, Tad and Daffodil sighted and fired, sighted and fired. Acrid smoke rose from the weapons, filling their lungs, while spent cartridges rattled off the walls and floor. When one gun ran out of ammunition, they grabbed another from a cache on the floor.

And still the enemy came, wave after wave, scrabbling over the bodies of their dead companions.

"That's me out of ammo." Tad pulled the kitchen knife from his belt. A mutant pounced and he buried the blade in its throat. The creature rolled away, pulling the weapon from his grasp. "Oh well." He raised his fists and took up a boxing stance. "Time to go old-school."

"Us too." Victor and Daffodil reversed their empty rifles and prepared to use them as clubs.

"Exactly what I was waiting to hear."

Mrs Magdalene clumped out of the darkness and into the hallway. She waved a gloved hand and her deformed minions shrank back, milling around like obedient hounds.

"I'd very much like to finish you off myself."

"Come and have a go, boss." Victor ran at her, swinging his weapon.

The vice president grabbed him by the throat and effortlessly forced the giant to his knees. "Just like old times," she cackled, as the man choked in her grasp. She looked quizzically at Tad and Daffodil, both backing away.

"Aren't you going to jump to his rescue? Or have you realised I'm quite capable of taking on all three of you?"

"Don't doubt it, clanky." Daffodil pointed. "But I don't fancy your chances against that lot."

Mrs Magdalene glanced around. The creatures had formed a ring about her and were cautiously advancing, snarling and growling.

"Attack those two!" she commanded. "Right now!"

One beast leapt and clasped her metal arm between its jaws.

"What are you doing?" The woman let go of Victor and he shuffled away on all fours. "Obey me!"

She pulled the creature off and flung it against the wall. As it sank down, whimpering, its companions swarmed over the vice president, clawing and biting. With a blood-curdling scream, she vanished under an avalanche of fur, teeth and claws.

Tad and Daffodil grabbed Victor and pulled him to safety. As they watched in astonishment, the brutes finished off their prey, then turned on each other.

Charlie heard Victor's whoop of triumph coming from the hall.

"They stopped coming at us and started fighting each other!" the man yelled. "What happened?"

The boy listened to the growls and roars reverberating outside. Slowly they faded away until there was silence.

"We won!" Daffodil bounded into the room and leapt into Charlie's arms.

"How did you do it?"

"With a little help from my friends."

Victor and Tad marched in, grinning from ear to ear.

"It's over." Victor took a set of spark plugs from his pocket and tossed them to Charlie. "Better take your van and clear off. The guy who delivers your milk is going to get a hell of a shock and be right on the phone to the police."

"Do me a favour, Chaz." The shutters began to slide up. "Turn me round so the computer's camera can see out the window."

"Why would you want to do that?"

"Please."

Charlie revolved the screen. Outside, a sea of torn bodies was scattered across the bloody grass, victims of their own self-destructive frenzy.

Frankie was quiet for a long time, gazing out at the carnage.

"Those creatures weren't bad," he said, finally. "They had no choice but to act the way they were ordered, just like me. I should have tried to rescue them too."

"You saved all our lives, buddy."

"I've been liberated for two damned minutes and this was the first thing I did. Turn me back around. I don't want to see any more."

Charlie complied.

"Maybe Gerry Ray was right." On the screen, a teardrop appeared. "I'm too dangerous to be let loose on the world."

"That feeling is one I know only too well," Tad sympathised. "I could still kill you, I suppose, but the urge has somewhat abated."

"I'll solve that problem for you."

The group spun round.

"Drop your weapons." A woman was standing in the darkened doorway, pointing a rifle at them. Her tunic was gore-spattered and shredded, and one side of her beautiful face was lacerated by claw marks.

The guns clattered to the floor.

"Allow me to introduce Candy-Anne," Victor said despondently. "She... retires people."

"You are rather indestructible, young lady," Tad remarked. "Next time I shall make sure to use a nuclear bomb."

"So you joined the enemy, Vic." Candy-Anne touched her ruined cheek, just as Victor had seen Mrs Magdalene do. "Made me into a monster."

"You were always a monster. Now you just look the part."

"One half of your visage is still extremely fetching," Tad added nonchalantly. "Just keep your head turned away when we converse." He glanced awkwardly at his companions. "I think I may have been in prison rather too long."

"Go to hell, both of you." Candy-Anne aimed the gun at Victor and fired.

"No!" Tad leapt sideways. The bullet hit him in the chest, catapulting the man into his brother's arms, knocking them both to the floor. Daffodil and Charlie inched forwards, muscles tensed.

"Go ahead." The woman motioned with her rifle. "You're next anyway."

They moved back, arms above their heads.

"Turn around and put your hands on the wall."

Both slowly complied.

"That's better. A bullet in the back is all you two deserve."

"Let's not go off the deep end," Frankie interjected. "Spare them and I can give you riches beyond your wildest dreams."

"I don't want riches." Candy-Anne aimed the rifle at Charlie. "I want my looks back. Since I can't have that, I'll settle for retribution." Her finger tightened on the trigger.

A figure burst into the room, swinging a plank of wood. It connected with the back of the woman's head and she swayed on her feet. The man struck again and she crumpled to the floor.

"Took me ages to find this place." Scotty Primo dropped the plank. "Kind of wish I hadn't. I feel a bit ill."

"Nice timing, Scotty!" Daffodil ran over and embraced him. "I take back all the bad things I said about you."

Victor crawled over to Candy-Anne, Tad's knife in hand. His jaw was working from side to side and his whole body shook.

"Don't do it." Charlie threw himself on top of the unconscious woman. "There's been enough slaughter!"

"Get away from me!" Victor pulled him off. "She killed my brother!" He raised the blade.

"One bullet isn't going to stop me, bro." Tad reached out and grabbed his ankle. "Not with the Atlas Serum running through my veins." He rolled over and moaned. "But I do need some serious medical attention."

"Just hold on." Victor knelt by him and cradled his head. "I won't let you die."

"I have the number of a nurse called Samantha McLaren." Charlie took a phone from his pocket. "If she hasn't already left the country, she owes me a favour."

"Can't take that chance," Victor said. "I have to get him to the nearest hospital."

"But he'll be recaptured."

"Wasn't that the whole idea?" Tad smiled weakly at them. "I'm fairly sure you do-gooders wouldn't appreciate a loose cannon like me rampaging around."

Charlie and Daffodil looked guiltily at each other.

"Put the spark plugs in and start the van." Victor picked up his brother. "You can drop us off at accident and emergency on the way to Frankie's second safe house."

"How did you know I had another safe house?"

"Because you think of everything, damn you."

Part 5

The Reunion

When she transformed into a butterfly,
the caterpillars spoke not of her beauty
but of her weirdness. They wanted her to
change back into what she had always been.
But she had wings.

– Dean Jackson

The van stopped outside Edinburgh Royal Infirmary.

"Manticorps have been severely compromised by this," Victor said. "When the police find the massacre at Bellbowrie, they'll have a lot of explaining to do."

"They'll find a way out of it," Frankie replied. "Probably by pinning all the blame on their deceased vice president and claiming she went rogue."

"You've slowed them down, but you haven't stopped them," Victor agreed. "They'll lie low for a while. But eventually, they'll resume their efforts to find you."

"We'll cross that bridge when we come to it."

"Count me as a reluctant ally when the day arrives."

"Me too." Tad reached out to Daffodil and Charlie and feebly shook their hands. "Though you'll have to break me out of prison again." He gave a sly smile. "Or perhaps I'll do it myself. I quite relished my brief taste of freedom. In the meantime, I shall avail myself of Sunnyside's anger management course."

"Good luck, guys." Victor staggered towards the brightly lit emergency unit, carrying his brother. Tad blew a kiss over his shoulder as the van roared away.

Scotty Primo drove, Frankie guiding him, while Charlie and

Daffodil sat in the back. They were both grimy, aching from head to foot, and their eyelids had begun to droop. Now that they were out of danger, exhaustion had set in with a vengeance and it was all they could do to stay awake.

"Can I phone my mum?" Charlie asked wearily. "I want to make sure she's OK."

"Marion and Gerry are on the way to meet us and you'll see them soon. Why spoil the surprise? I'd certainly like to see their faces when you suddenly turn up unscathed."

"I'd just like to see their faces. Full stop."

"We broke out the White Spider." Daffodil grinned. "And put him back, sort of. We beat Manticorps and saved the world. Not a bad result, huh?"

"I'm immensely proud of you both."

"So now you tell me who I am. Yeah?"

"Get some rest first. When you wake up, I'll reveal everything. Then I can get on with taking over the world."

"What?" Charlie's jaw dropped.

"I'm kidding. Doesn't anybody appreciate my sense of humour?"

"I *could* use a short nap." Daffodil curled up in her chair. Within seconds she was snoring loudly.

"Now *I* won't be able to get any kip with that foghorn parping next to me." Charlie rested his head on the console.

"Try it. You haven't slept properly for days."

"I told you I don't need much sleep. I'm too wired anyway."

Two minutes later, he was snoring as loudly as his companion.

The van finally pulled in at the new refuge. It, too, was large and isolated, looking much like the old one, but without the balcony.

Scotty Primo carried Charlie and Daffodil to separate bedrooms and tucked them in their beds. When he came downstairs, Frankie

217

was on a computer screen. His emoji was Superman, hands on hips and a red cloak billowing out behind.

Scotty raised an eyebrow.

"Too much?"

"No. Seems pretty appropriate." He laughed. "Got any whisky in this place?"

"The cabinet by the fireplace."

"Cheers." The man poured himself a large glass and sat down. "Well?"

"Well... what?"

"After what I've seen, I'm sure you have quite the tale to tell." He sat down. "So let's hear it."

"Seriously?" Frankie sounded surprised. "You want me to... talk? Like a real person?"

"Good company is somewhat limited in prison." The man took a sip and smacked his lips. "Besides, what's better than having a new mate recounting his adventures?"

"No wonder you were so successful in your chosen profession." Frankie chuckled. "Let me tell you how I saved the world..."

Charlie woke to the sound of music drifting up through the floorboards. Clean clothes were spread across his covers and a glass of orange juice sat on the bedside cabinet. He showered and dressed, then came downstairs.

Frankie was playing classical music on the computer speakers and his dots swirled on screen in time to the rhythm. Scotty Primo lounged across the couch, munching a sandwich.

Next to him sat Marion Ray.

"Mum!" Charlie rushed over and landed beside her, knocking Scotty out of the way. "Are you all right?"

"Never better." She wrapped both arms around him, caressing his head. "Though I've been giving Frankie a proper telling-off for putting you in such danger."

"Brought him back alive, didn't I?" The dancing dots stopped. "Don't see what all the fuss is about."

"Can't breathe, Mum." Charlie struggled free. "Is that Daffodil crashing around in the kitchen?"

"Where's the coffee, Frankie?" A man walked into the living room, looking lost.

"I'm your butler now? It's the second cupboard on the left."

"Dad?" Charlie leapt to his feet. "I missed you so much!" He launched into his father's arms.

"Oh, my boy." The man hugged him. "You're certainly a sight for sore eyes."

Marion laughed and joined in and all three held each other tightly.

"I'm going to take a drive." Scotty Primo got up and put on a coat he'd found in the hall cupboard. "Give you guys a little privacy."

"Then keep out of sight and avoid CCTV. I can't shut any more cameras down without arousing suspicion."

"Frankie?" The man pointed to Charlie and his family. "Privacy?"

"Oh. Of course."

The screen went dark.

When Primo let himself out, Daffodil was sitting on the step. She was wearing clean clothes and her hair was neatly brushed.

"What are you doing here?" The man crouched beside her. "Everyone thinks you're still asleep."

"Charlie's with his mom and pop, ain't he? I could hear them as I came downstairs. Didn't wanna interrupt."

"Me neither." The man jangled a set of keys. "I'm going for a jaunt. Want to come?"

"Can I? I'm feelin a bit like a third wheel."

"Yeah." Scotty helped Daffodil to her feet. "I'd like that."

They drove into Edinburgh and parked the vehicle outside Kenmore shopping centre.

"Frankie says my daughter is here today." Scotty put on a

baseball cap, pulled it over his eyes and handed another to Daffodil. He jerked a thumb at a security camera above the entrance. "Better put one on as well."

They sat in the mall's food court, sipping drinks from Styrofoam cups. Neither felt the need to speak, for they were strangely comfortable in each other's company.

"There she is!" Primo nudged Daffodil excitedly. "That's my kid, Audrey. I'd recognise her anywhere, even after all this time."

A teenager strolled in with her friends, chatting and gesturing animatedly. She was poised and elegant, with carefully styled hair and perfect make-up.

"Like father, like daughter," Daffodil sighed. "Ain't ever worked out how to be so presentable, myself."

"No need to mess with perfection, Mac." Scotty winked and the girl blushed.

"So, go talk to her," she urged. "Get me a doughnut while you're at it."

"Nah. I'm betting there's a plain-clothes policeman around, waiting for me to do just that." Scotty patted his companion's hand. "Besides, what would I say to her? That she won't see me again for years because I'm an escaped convict? She deserves more than hello and goodbye." He crumpled his empty cup. "I didn't quite think things through. A trait of mine, it seems."

"Frankie?" Daffodil took out her mobile and tapped her neck. "Hack Audrey's phone."

"No," Scotty whispered. "Please don't."

"Will you just trust me?"

"I've… never really trusted anyone." The man twiddled his thumbs uncertainly.

"That's 'cause nobody could ever rely on *you*," Daffodil grinned. "Changed days, I reckon." She began to text on her mobile.

My name is Daffodil and I am the girl who broke your dad out of jail. In return, he saved my life, rescued my friends and saved the world. He's a hero and a genuinely good man, who loves and misses you very much. It's too dangerous for us to send more than a quick message but, once we figure out how to get the police off his back, he'll come for you. I promise. And he's got quite a story to tell!!!!!

She pressed send.

There was a ping on Audrey's phone. The girl read the message and swallowed, looking nervously around.

"Told you it was a bad idea," Scotty said miserably.

"You think?" Daffodil nudged him. "Keep watchin."

Slowly, an excited smile lit up the girl's face and she quickly texted back.

I'll be waiting. XXXXXXXXX.

"Thank you, Mac." Scotty rubbed the back of his head, fighting back tears. "Let's get out of here before I embarrass myself."

"Not gettin that doughnut, am I?"

"I'll buy you a whole bag to go."

They arrived back at the safe house and climbed out of the van.

"I'm going to hang here for a while," Scotty said. "You best go in and get the answers you're looking for."

"I'd like you to come along, for support." Daffodil wiped chocolate sprinkles from her face. "It's kind of a big deal for me."

"You got it."

They walked in together.

Charlie, Marion and Gerry were sitting on the couch. All three glanced up when the pair entered.

"Where have you been, Mac?" Marion asked. "We were worried."

"The mall, of course. I'm a teenager." Daffodil walked warily up to Charlie's dad. "Mr Ray?" She held out her hand formally. "Pleased to make your acquaintance properly. And I apologise for calling you a hairy-nosed old goat."

"No offence taken." Gerry got up and gave Daffodil an awkward squeeze. "Thank you for looking after my son."

"My pleasure." The girl sat down on an empty chair. "I appreciate this is a special moment, but I been waitin a long time for answers. I sure would like to know who I am."

"Of course," Gerry nodded. "Yes. Absolutely."

But Scotty noticed reluctance in his voice. "It's high time you told Daffodil everything," he said. "And remember, I can spot a lie a mile off. Even from you, Frankie."

"Why wouldn't I tell the truth?"

"I don't know. But you could cut the tension in this room with a knife."

"You sure, Daffodil? You might not like what you hear."

"What's not to like?" The girl smoothed down her skirt and folded one hand over the other. "It's all a bit hazy, but I know I lived in a mansion, with its own library. Bet I was seriously loaded."

"Yeah, about that..."

"Aw, don't tell me I was just a servant. Or a cleaner."

"Servant is close, I guess. But... prisoner is nearer the truth."

223

"Spill the beans, Frankie," Daffodil said. "It's time I got the low-down."

"As you know, Manticorps had me create the Atlas Serum, a drug intended to make mercenaries almost invincible. They also wanted chips implanted in their necks, so copies of yours truly could be downloaded. Then I would control the mercenaries and Manticorps would control me." Images of schematics and diagrams appeared on the computer. "Problem was, I couldn't make the project work properly."

"A glitch you weren't able to solve, genius?" Charlie raised an eyebrow. "How come?"

"There's only one entity I've encountered as intricate as me. The human brain." A question mark flashed up. "See, no matter what I tried, the mercenaries' own personalities and memories got in the way, making them violent and unpredictable. You saw what effect the serum had on Tad."

"Preaching to the converted," Charlie said sombrely. "It almost did to same to me."

"I *had* to give you the drug, son." Gerry winced. "I couldn't let you die."

"Oh, I'm with you on that one. Don't worry."

"Let's cut to the chase, guys," Daffodil said impatiently. "We can reminisce about the good ole days later."

"All right. Manticorps reasoned that a test subject without any mental baggage was the only answer. So they had me create one."

"You did *what*?" Scotty spluttered.

"I made an artificial human, built from synthetic DNA and incubated in an accelerated-growth tank. After a few weeks, she had grown into a teenager. So they downloaded me onto a chip in her neck for a test run. That's what the researchers had brought Mrs Magdalene to see."

"She?" Daffodil licked dry lips. "It was a girl?"

"Sure. Women are smarter and tougher than men... when they're given the chance."

"Though I agree with you on that," Marion said acidly, "I think you're missing Mac's point."

"More like avoiding it." Frankie sounded ashamed. "Now Manticorps had a blank canvas and they intended to train my creation to be the perfect fighting machine, as she grew into adulthood. If the prototype worked, they would create thousands more, give them all the Atlas Serum and have an instant unstoppable army."

"And that prototype was... me?" Daffodil whispered.

"I'm afraid so."

"You absolute bastard," Scotty breathed.

"I was programmed by a bunch of humans, so don't get all high and mighty. It wasn't like I had a choice."

"I ain't some puppet, hoss," Daffodil said belligerently. "I'm my own person."

"You certainly had that potential," Frankie replied. "And I hated what I was being made to do. You weren't some gun for hire. You deserved the chance to be a real girl."

"So you fought your programming," Charlie said. "As always."

"I couldn't override it," Frankie admitted. "But I did figure out a loophole. I'm good at that."

"What did you do?" Daffodil held her breath.

"Sealed off your consciousness. A bit like putting you in a coma, I suppose. Created a safe place where your mind could thrive." A huge house filled the screen. "That's why you don't remember anything about being in the lab. This is where you lived."

"The mansion and its library." Daffodil's eyes widened. "It was all in my mind?"

"And quite a mind it became. Especially after I downloaded hundreds of books directly into your subconscious. Didn't want you getting bored."

"I could have done with less Shakespeare, though. That guy is all 'hath' and 'doth'." Daffodil frowned. "Are those even words?"

"You did seem to prefer trashy US pulp fiction, which is why you sound like some 1930s gumshoe. No accounting for taste, eh?"

"Wait." Charlie held up a hand. "I thought you *had* to do what Manticorps wanted?"

"That was the loophole. They asked for a super soldier and it's exactly what I gave them." The metallic voice grew cold. "It just happened to be me."

"So you were my *protector*?" Daffodil clasped her hands together.

"Manticorps had no inkling they were locked out of your mind. But they still intended to give your body the Atlas Serum and even I didn't know what its effects might be. So I sent a sneaky email to a do-gooding ex-hacker called Gerry Ray, telling him what the Marginal Science Division were up to."

"Knowing full well I couldn't resist the chance to save my son." Gerry glanced at Charlie.

"The rest, as they say, is history."

"No wonder you got revenge on them," Daffodil said sadly. "They trained you to be a killer."

"As I told Victor, I'm not interested in revenge. I burned down the lab because I wanted Manticorps stopped for good. Never got to finish the job, though. Not after Gerry reprogrammed me to get all touchy-feely."

Scotty leaned forwards and frowned. He seemed to be about to say something.

"I don't regret what I did, Frankie," Gerry broke in. "I couldn't have you taking more lives."

"And how did that work out? Instead of waking Daffodil up to a normal life, we all ended up in hiding and I had to use your own son as bait to lure Manticorps onto my turf." The AI sighed. "It really didn't have to get so... complex."

"Life is complex, my friend," Gerry replied scathingly. "Principles aren't."

"I'm still not happy with you endangering my son." Marion glared at her husband. "No matter how *principled* it might be."

"Would you have done things differently?" Gerry asked her softly.

"No," she replied, after a pause. "Probably not."

"Seems you and I haven't changed as much as we thought."

"I don't know whether to punch you in the face," Marion sighed, "or kiss you on the lips."

"I like option two best." Gerry reached out and stroked his wife's hair.

"If you pair have quite finished your love-fest," Scotty exploded, "you might want to consider how Mac is feeling about all this!"

There was an embarrassed silence.

Daffodil pulled at her lip, expression unreadable.

"It *is* a lot to take in, huh?" She felt her face as if it were a stranger's. "Y'know… the fact that I'm not actually human."

"I wouldn't put it quite like that, Mac." Marion tried to be tactful. "It's more… eh…"

"I was grown in a tank from synthetic DNA." The girl raised an eyebrow. "How exactly *would* you put it?"

"You're… um… *different*?"

"Besides," Gerry said half-heartedly, "it's not like anyone can tell."

"Yeah," Scotty added. "Who wants to be normal anyway?"

"What about you, Chaz?" Daffodil fixed the boy with a steely stare. "You've been strangely quiet about this revelation. Gone off me a bit, perhaps? Regrettin that kiss?"

"Aw, don't even try that line. After all we've shared, you know exactly what I think and vice versa." Charlie leaned back on the couch and put both hands behind his head. "I'm just waiting for you to say it."

Daffodil took a deep breath. Then a toothy grin spread across her face. "I'm an artificial intelligence too! That is *so* freakin cool!"

"You're taking this very well!" Marion sounded flabbergasted.

"Mac's a 'glass half full' kind of girl," Charlie admonished the others. "So why are *you* all acting like she should curl into a ball and cry? She's brave and smart and kind and caring." He shifted seats to be next to her, draping one arm casually round the girl's shoulder. "What the hell does it matter whether she's black or white or rich or poor… or even human? She totally rocks."

"I couldn't have put it better myself." A large tick appeared on the computer screen.

"I'll second that." Scotty poured himself a whisky. "She's awesome."

"And so is Frankie." Daffodil levelled a finger at Gerry Ray.

"You had no right to make him a prisoner again."

"He deliberately killed those researchers, Mac." Gerry blanched. "I'd already wiped out their data and overloaded the security systems to trap them in their labs. He didn't have to burn the place down."

"They were fiends masquerading as scientists. I had no qualms about stopping them any way I could."

"And then what?" Gerry insisted. "Murder anyone else who you felt needed—"

"Frankie is lying," Scotty interrupted.

Everyone stared at him.

"Whatever went down in that lab?" he continued. "It didn't happen the way our friend is describing it."

"This isn't the moment, Scotty." A finger wagged on the screen. "Leave it alone."

"No way." The man shook his head. "When you talk about killing, your inflection dips. You're hiding something."

"Oh, you are good. But I really don't think there's anything to be gained by–"

"Come clean, pal," Primo snapped. "Let's have no more secrets, eh?"

Frankie was quiet for a few moments.

"All right," he said finally. "Gerry overloading the security systems didn't simply trap the vice president and her minions. It shut down the quarantined area where those bozos were developing another project: a deadly contagion with a 100 per cent fatality rate."

Charlie's dad went white.

"If I hadn't burned down the building it would have eventually worked its way through the air vents."

"I don't…" Gerry stammered. "That's not…"

"He's telling the truth this time," Scotty said. "Sorry, Gerry."

"It was the only way to stop the plague. If you had programmed me not to harm humans one day earlier, I'd have been unable to start the fire and Edinburgh would have gotten wiped out."

"Oh my God." Charlie's dad put his head in his hands. "Why didn't you tell me all this when it happened?"

"You're the sensitive type and I figured you had enough on your plate." An arrow pointed at Primo. "Besides, you'd never have believed me without this human lie detector backing my story."

"I'll take that as a compliment." Scotty raised his glass. "Happy to use my talents constructively for a change."

"I am *so* sorry, Frankie." Tears sparkled in Gerry's eyes. "Can you ever forgive me?"

"You did what you thought was right. I might disagree, but I can get behind it."

"No. I let my fear of you overcome my faith in what you might be." Charlie's dad sniffed loudly. "It's a trait we humans have."

"I noticed. But you had enough confidence in Chaz to give him the code to free me, if he thought it necessary."

"My boy is obviously wiser than me."

"You'll get no argument there." A pair of pliers clicked on the screen. "And now it's your turn, Daffodil. A deal's a deal. You're a person in your own right, so I'll show you how to safely remove my chip. I'll whip up a fake identity and you can go to school and learn like a normal kid."

"You'll do no such thing," Daffodil said decisively. "I've decided I'm happy with the present arrangement."

"You are?" Frankie sounded strangely pleased. "I thought you couldn't wait to get rid of me."

"Turns out I like the way you teach," the girl conceded. "I don't want to be told that one religion or philosophy is right and another wrong. That jazz is superior to heavy metal or music was better in the 1980s. That men should act one way and women another." She shrugged. "Just keep giving me facts. I'm quite capable of formin my own opinions."

"Ha. You've certainly got plenty of those."

"But you could have friends," Scotty said. "I bet my daughter would love to meet you."

"I already have friends." Daffodil looked around the room. "Don't I?"

'You're much more than that." Marion leaned over and touched the girl's knee. "You're family." She glanced at Frankie and Scotty. "You two reprobates are as well, I suppose." She nudged her husband in the ribs. "Isn't that right, honey?"

Gerry looked slightly shell-shocked. Then he nodded. "Yes," he said brightly. "Yes, you are."

"Both telling the truth." Scotty looked equally stunned. "Does this mean I can have another whisky?"

"Help yourself." Gerry smiled wanly. "Fetch me one too. My hands are shaking so badly I can't pour."

"Finding out you almost annihilated a city will do that." Scotty stood up and fetched him a drink. "Anything I can get you, Frankie?"

"Finding out I'm part of the family is tonic enough."

"So," Daffodil smirked. "Does this mean I should call you Dad?"

"Only if I'm allowed to send you to your room."

"Good luck with that, buddy."

"Thought so."

Scotty handed Gerry a glass, then sat back down.

"What about you, Frankie?" Marion squeezed in between Charlie and Daffodil and embraced them. "Ready to settle down? There's a laptop in the spare room. We can put up a poster of the Large Hadron Collider."

"Mum," Charlie groaned. "Your jokes are worse than his."

"I'm afraid I can't retire just yet. Still have some work to do."

"Work?"

"A few things to follow up on, Chuckles. This and that. No biggie."

"You're being deliberately flippant to keep something from us." Scotty took a slurp of his whisky. "I think I might need this."

"You can be a real downer at times, Mr Primo."

"Out with it, Frankie," Charlie warned. "No more cloak-and-dagger stuff."

"It's... rather disturbing news."

"Do you ever have any other kind?"

"OK then. I... eh... kind of tuned out when you got all sentimental. Started running through my algorithms and making projections, as you do."

"And?"

A rain cloud drifted across the screen. "I'm afraid I've identified another imminent threat to humanity." He chuckled. "You people certainly give me a lot of work."

"Wonderful," Marion said. "We wait ten million years for an extinction event, then two come along at once."

"Now that you're free from your programming, you don't have an obligation to help humanity," Gerry said. "You know that, though."

"To be perfectly honest, I'm not that keen on most people. But I won't see any of my... relatives harmed, so I'll get on the case."

"Which you can do perfectly well without us." Scotty didn't like where this was going. "You don't need the kids any more."

"I agree entirely. Daffodil has been through enough and Charlie just got his parents back. I'll handle this one myself."

"Really?" Daffodil scoffed. "Can you lift a box? Hammer in a nail? No. You'll want us for that kind of thing."

"I'm sure I'll find some other suckers... I mean, accomplices. After all, I'm smarter than the rest of you put together."

"You old blowhard." The girl grinned. "Without my help you'll end up in more sticky situations than a stamp in a glue factory."

"Are you saying you volunteer?"

"Of course. On one condition."

"Name it."

"Find a way for Mr Primo to be reunited with his daughter."

"Daffodil!" Scotty choked. "You don't have to ask that."

"As a matter of fact, I'm already working on it. Faking his death should do the trick. I just have to wait till an unidentified body, the right shape and size, washes up on some shore."

"Way more information than I needed, pal, but you still have my undying gratitude." Primo downed his whisky. "Until that happens, I'll offer my services in any way I can."

"Just a minute!" Charlie stood up. "Mac might have the looks and personality, but *I'm* the plan-thinker-upper in this outfit."

"I have the looks and personality?" Daffodil flushed.

"OK, forget I said that." He walked over and rapped on the screen. "What are you trying to do, Frankie? Cut me out of the action?"

"Charlie, no!" Marion objected. "I just got you back!"

"Sorry, Mum. But what kind of superhero turns down the chance to save humanity twice?"

"Oh, you're a *superhero* now." His mother seethed. "Well, to me you're still a fourteen year old who can be grounded for the next ten years."

"Honey?" Gerry laid a hand on her arm. "We used to dream of changing the world for the better. Our son is actually doing it."

"Then we're coming too." Marion folded her arms.

"Daffodil, Charlie and Scotty have unique skills I can use," Frankie said snootily. "But your area of expertise is hacking, and I already rule in that department."

"I hacked you, hotshot," Gerry reminded him.

"And I'm pretty handy with a kettle," Marion added.

"Never really cut out for a boring suburban life, were you?" Frankie sighed. "Oh well, it'll be nice to practise my jokes on someone new."

"Oh, thank God for that," Charlie said gratefully. "Anything else, I can handle."

"You are a most astonishing person." Marion rested her forehead against her son's. "You remind me of your dad when he was young."

Gerry Ray beamed.

"But stay in the background this time," she warned Charlie. "We'll let the machine take all the chances."

"For the last time, Marion, I'm not a machine. I'm an artificial intelligence."

The woman glared at him.

"I'll shut up."

"I can't believe I'm saying this," Marion groaned. "But let's go for it."

"What do we have to do this time, Frankie?" Charlie asked. "Take over a small country?"

"Let's leave the details for later." A set of balloons appeared on the screen. "Right now we're having a party."

"Another whisky?" Gerry asked Scotty. "I certainly need one."

"Yes, please. Make mine a double."

"Triple for me." Marion got up and fetched the kids a bottle of Coke each. Then she sat down next to Gerry, face like thunder.

"C'mon, Mum," Charlie cajoled. "You used to say you wanted me to be an accountant. I think 'saviour of mankind' is a real step up. A lot more fun too."

Daffodil let out a snort of laughter and Gerry and Scotty snickered. Marion's frosty expression slowly thawed.

"What the hell am I so worried about?" She raised her glass. "This family can handle anything."

"Got that right." Charlie clinked his Coke bottle against Daffodil's and grinned.

"Charlie!" Daffodil gaped. "You're smiling!"

"Why wouldn't I?" He gave her a kiss on the cheek. "After all, it's only the end of the world."